CHAPTER
1

LYALL

The Draugur threw itself headlong across the rooftop, attempting to barrel into Lyall and knock him off his feet.

Breathing heavily, Lyall turned away from the body of the creature that he had just killed, twisting and stepping to the side at the same time. He just managed to avoid the grotesque figure as it flew past him, howling and salivating before toppling over the edge of the rooftop with a startled cry.

Lyall took a moment to cross the roof, and peered over the lip to the street below. The Draugur had hit the ground sixty feet down and basically split apart like a melon.

There would have been a time—not very long ago—he would have been concerned about humans seeing the body of the Draugur. Unfortunately, humans were more than used to seeing both live and dead Draugur these days, as Sluag sent ever more of his rogue souls through the veil to steal innocent people's bodies.

Finally, free from attack, he turned to watch his companion, and a smile hooked his lip up at the side. He couldn't help it; she was the most fierce and beautiful thing he had ever seen.

Flora was wrestling with a Draugur, and where he once would have panicked and run to help her, he took this moment to stand back and watch her work.

She was on her back, having just been knocked to the ground by the thing, which was now leaning over her, snapping and snarling in her face—Sluag no longer seemed concerned with getting Flora to the Endwood to kill her, since the veil was fracturing a little more each day anyway.

It had been eight months since the Dion and the Soul Keeper had first heard reports of the rogue souls breaking into the mortal world, and they were now extremely used to dealing with the Draugur daily.

Flora and her Dion had managed to keep the flow of Draugur down by sending out constant patrols to deal with them, just like the one they were on tonight. Fortunately, because these Draugur were created in a slightly different way, they were much easier to kill than Sluag's Endwood creations.

Their souls had never been to the Endwood, so the stolen body could be killed by using usual methods, which would in turn cast the rogue soul out into the mortal world where it would remain trapped in limbo forever.

This gave the Dion the added bonus of not needing Flora's

SOUL ETERNAL

EVERWOOD TRILOGY 3

KATE KEIR

SOUL ETERNAL
Copyright © 2018 Kate Keir
All rights reserved.

DEDICATION

For my amazing nephew &
three beautiful nieces.
I love you! xxx

energy to obliterate the rogue souls, so they could all hunt the new Draugur.

It was a relief for Lyall because it meant that Flora didn't have to constantly put herself at risk by continual energy use.

A grunt from the Draugur brought Lyall's attention back to the present as he watched Flora kick the monster hard in the stomach. The creature rolled backward, caught off balance. Flora took the opportunity to jump to her feet and bring her sword down in a smooth arc that pierced the Draugur's chest and allowed the rogue soul to escape with a burst of blue fire into its permanent limbo.

He clapped his hands and smiled. "Well done, love."

She turned to him, her green eyes lit by the fire of battle, and she beamed. "Thanks, you didn't do so bad yourself." She panted through ragged breath.

His throat tightened, and his heart hurt as she stayed several feet away from him to catch her breath.

Lyall had eventually realised his stupidity in holding her kiss with Finlay against her. He would have done the exact same thing in her shoes and he had apologised to Flora for being a complete ass.

She had accepted his apology, and they had moved forward from that day, they were a bonded couple, after all, and that could not be undone.

Yet, things felt different between them. Some days she would throw herself into his arms, kissing him so hard he worried they would die for lack of air. Other days—like today—

she would seem distant and untouchable.

Not for the first time, he wondered if they would ever be able to get back to where they had been before her kiss with Finlay.

She often went to see Finlay in the Everwood, and she would always seem so sad when she returned. Lyall knew that Finlay was living on borrowed time. Eventually, Flora would have to admit she couldn't give him the body he needed, and he would ask her to send him into oblivion.

Lyall was pretty sure that day was going to break her apart, and he was scared it would break their relationship completely too. He just didn't know how to help her through it.

He knew he was a complete idiot to be jealous of a soul, but he was, and he knew Flora sensed his envy and resented him for it. They never spoke about it, though, because they had so many bigger things to deal with.

They were no closer to finding a way to close the veil, Sluag had created more Super Draugur, and the Dion still had no idea how to kill them. Their cause felt more desperate with every passing day.

He also knew that Flora grew more afraid with every day that brought her closer to her twenty-first birthday. She still hadn't been betrayed, and with only three months until her big day, he knew she was convinced she would be dead before long.

Watching her standing on the roof of the multi-storey carpark as she finally got her breath back and straightened up, he felt a familiar ache in his chest. If he lost her, he knew he would die too. There was no point to his life unless Flora was there by his side. He just wished he could tell her how he felt.

"We should get out of here. The police are probably already on their way," she called to him.

Surveying the bodies which littered the rooftop, Lyall smiled grimly. "Agreed, let's get out of here, love."

They both raced for the green exit sign that led to the lower levels of the carpark. Flora had long since grown tired of trying to get Draugur blood out of her clothes, instead insisting on wearing all black for their hunting expeditions. In another lifetime, Lyall would have thought it was kind of cute that they matched.

They sped around the corner of level three, and Lyall crashed into Flora's back as she skidded to a halt in front of him. His wandering mind snapped back to the present as Flora hissed, "Super Draugur."

Two of the monstrosities were slinking through the shadows across the carpark. They were so unconcerned with the public seeing them that they didn't bother to disguise their hideous, rotting features. They were dressed in grey armour that was a simple version of the clothing that Sluag always wore.

Swearing under his breath, Lyall wrapped his arm around Flora's waist and pulled her back into the shadows on their side of the carpark, hoping they hadn't been spotted. Because they had no way of killing Super Draugur, provoking a fight was pointless.

Too late. One of the Super Draugur turned its head toward

them and hissed through its broken, yellowed teeth. "Ssoul Keeper? I ssee you and your bonded Dion."

They started to slowly approach, and Lyall burst forward from the shadows, pulling Flora along by her wrist. "Run, love," he shouted.

CHAPTER 2

FLORA

I stumbled as Lyall pulled me across the carpark behind him. Despite the danger from the Super Draugur, I still felt a tingle of electricity burn through my wrist as his fingers touched my bare skin.

Every single fibre of my being told me this man would love and protect me for eternity. *He was the one.*

Yet, you wouldn't think it, over the last few months. One minute we were up, and the next we were down. It was mainly due to my relationship with Finlay, I knew. Lyall just didn't understand that my love for Finlay was purely platonic.

No matter what else happened, I would never stop trying to find a way to give Finlay a permanent body; he didn't deserve to be trapped in the Everwood in the way he was right now.

My foot suddenly landed at a strange angle as I stepped down onto the road, and I yelped in pain and yanked my arm back from Lyall.

"Flora, are you all right? Have you damaged it?" He shot a worried look over my shoulder, and I followed his gaze in time to see the two Super Draugur appear at the open front of the carpark. As soon as they spotted us, they began to approach us with hungry looks on their faces.

Sluag had made Lyall and I number one priority with all of his Draugur since he had discovered our bond. Pen had agreed that it was likely if one of us died, then the other would probably follow shortly after. Either that or go mad with grief.

When I asked Pen why she hadn't died after losing Aiden, she had gone quiet before telling me she had been mad with grief for a long time after. It was simply the desire to protect all of us, that gave her the strength to go on.

"Flora?" Lyall's voice had a warning tone. We needed to move.

Giving my ankle a final quick rub, I stood and nodded at him. "I'm okay, let's go."

We bolted across the street and around a corner before flying across a surprisingly quiet street. I sent a silent *thank you* to whoever or whatever had made sure there were no cars on the road to hinder our progress.

"I don't wanna lead them back to Castle Dion, Flora. We need to outrun them before we head back." Lyall's voice came out in short gasps as we continued to run at full pelt.

I nodded my agreement, afraid to try to talk since I already felt as though my lungs were about to burst. After a year of Soul

Keeper training, I was fitter now than I had ever been before, but I still grew tired when I was running for my life.

Crossing the bridge over the River Ness and slipping into a shadowy park, we both pressed our backs against a wide-trunked tree that blocked us from view of the street and tried to breathe quietly as we waited for the Super Draugur to hopefully pass us by.

The creatures arrived soon after, and I bit my lip as I waited for them to either realise we were hiding or carry on past us, allowing us to retreat back to the castle.

I felt Lyall wrap his fingers through my own and squeeze my hand gently. I knew I should have felt comforted by his touch, but it just reminded me of how much I missed our closeness.

Our hiding place was well chosen; the Super Draugur didn't even hesitate before passing us by and disappearing along the street. I let out the breath I had been holding and tilted my head back against the tree trunk in relief.

After quickly double-checking they had definitely gone, Lyall signalled to me that we should leave. I didn't hesitate; I left the cover of the tree and followed my Dion to the place we had left our car. Once we were inside, and on our way back to the castle, I felt relief flood through me.

Lyall drove in silence, but his jaw was clenched ever so slightly, and I could tell he was thinking hard about something.

"What are you thinking about?" I hoped that I would catch him off-guard and manage to get an honest answer.

He shook his head dismissively. "Just wondering if we'll ever find a way to kill Supers, love."

I narrowed my eyes. "No, you weren't. Tell me the truth."

He was silent for so long I was certain he wasn't going to speak to me again before we got home.

Then finally, he said something. "Truthfully, Flora, I was just wondering how me and you have let things get so broken between us."

His words were not entirely unexpected, but that didn't make them hurt any less. I looked down at my hands. They were bloodstained and clasped tightly together on my lap. "I don't know," I whispered.

"You know that I love you, Flora."

"I love you too." It was the easiest thing I had said to him in a long time.

"But I don't feel as though I can compete with Finlay," he finished.

I felt my temper flare and fought to keep a lid on it.

"Lyall, do you remember when we first met?"

He frowned. "Of course, I do."

I nodded. "Finlay told me that he had spent his whole life protecting me and waiting for me to get to the point where I had to choose. He said that he had always expected me to choose him and that he had never expected to have to compete with you."

Lyall's amber eyes burned in the darkness. "What are you saying, love?"

I growled in frustration as I realised he had drawn the

wrong conclusion yet again. It was as though we had been speaking different languages over the last few months.

"I'm saying that there never was a competition. I never, ever wanted to be with Finlay in that way. Yes, my soul responded when he kissed me because he's my closest friend, and our history goes back so far. I can even admit that I enjoyed kissing him. But it was a goodbye kiss. I know I'm losing him, Lyall, and it breaks my heart every day to know it."

He started to speak, but I lifted my hand and cut him off.

"No, Lyall. I'm tired of your jealousy and doubt. You need to believe me when I tell you that I love you, and that no one makes me feel as safe and loved as I feel when I'm with you, really with you.

"All those months ago, Finlay asked me to choose because he thought it was a competition too. I chose back then, and my decision is still the same today. I chose you, Lyall, you just never realised it."

He hit the brakes so hard I nearly hit my head against the dashboard, despite my seatbelt. Swerving the car off the road and up onto a grass verge, he clicked his own seatbelt off and then opened his door to get out.

"Out," he barked at me.

Raising my eyebrows, I felt a tiny glimmer of fear as I rushed to oblige. His face was dark and gave nothing away as I stepped out of the car and turned to face him.

Without hesitation, he crossed the distance between us and crushed his lips against mine. He wrapped his strong arms around my waist and pulled my whole body against him.

I could have cried with relief as I melted against him, twining my arms around his neck and kissing him back with everything I had.

"I love you, I love you, I love you," I murmured against his mouth.

Pulling back from me, he gently grasped my face in both of his hands. "I love you too. I'm so sorry, Flora."

Then, dropping to his knees, he bowed his head and grasped my hands in his own. "I swear, I'll be a better protector and a better Dion. I will be everything you need and everything you deserve from now on."

Then he stood and kissed me again, and I felt my body and mind fill with complete elation—I had my Dion back.

CHAPTER
3

After we had rediscovered each other, I didn't want to let go of Lyall, and I was certain he felt the same way. We walked through the main door of Castle Dion with our fingers tightly entwined, and both of us were beaming.

Freya was just sauntering down the stairs as we walked in, and she rolled her eyes dramatically. "Urgh, as disgusting as that is, I'm glad you've both finally got a grip and sorted things out."

Bear followed behind Freya, and he grinned widely and waved hello to us both. "Glad to see you and your girl on form again, Lyall." Then to Freya, "See, that could be me and you if only you weren't such an ice queen, hotness."

"Urgh." Freya shot him a look that could kill and stormed into the dining hall.

Bear shrugged and winked at Lyall before following Freya in to the dining hall, muttering, "Women."

Lyall and I looked at each other and burst into laughter as we followed the others. I was always hungry after a night of hunting Draugur and I was grateful we had made it back home in time for breakfast.

Pen was seated at the wooden table when we walked in, and her eyes lit in delight when she saw how close I was to Lyall. We sat down next to each other and started to pick at the food.

"How went your night, you two?" Artair asked.

"Okay, although we did run into two Supers at the very end," Lyall replied.

"We ran into a Super too." Although Enid was talking to us, she didn't tear her gaze away from Artair. The two were inseparable these days, after announcing they were *official* around two months ago.

Pen sighed. "They become ever more frequent. I'd love to know how many Sluag has now."

"I'd like to know how much of Finlay's blood he has left." Leah was still the quietest of us, only ever speaking when she felt as though she really had something relevant to say.

"Have you seen nothing, Leah?" Pen quizzed the seer.

The blonde-haired girl shook her head grimly. "Nope, sorry."

Lyall shifted in his seat next to me. "He can't have very much of Finlay's blood left. Which means he'll be looking to take another Dion soon. We need to be extra careful when we're out on patrol."

Everyone nodded their agreement.

Pen studied Lyall for a moment, as if trying to decide if now was a good time to broach a particular topic. Seeming to make her decision, she spoke. "Talking of Finlay, I have been doing some reading, and I think that I might have a suggestion for trying to get him housed inside our pet."

Pet, was the term we had all adopted for the Super Draugur we kept in the cellars. I had tried over and over to dislodge its soul but hadn't come close to succeeding. We had even managed to feed it my blood, but its reaction was nothing like the ordinary Draugur. It had laughed at us and sworn that one day it would tear me apart when it escaped.

It couldn't be killed, and it couldn't be turned by my blood. We were at a complete loss.

So, I raised my eyebrows in surprise at Pen's statement. "What have you found, Pen?"

"I was thinking about the way the rogues steal human bodies from their pure soul owners in the mortal world. They literally fight their way inside and throw the pure souls out. I was wondering if you might have enough power if Finlay pushed and you pulled, Flora."

Freya was trying her best to ignore Bear's lovesick gaze. "I thought we couldn't kick its soul out because it belonged in there."

"It's the same principle as the pure souls. They shouldn't be able to be evicted by the rogues. I think whomever has the most power, will eventually win." Pen sounded confident.

Lyall sat back in his chair, his fingers still twisted through my own. "You want me to feed Flora my energy while she does it, right?"

I bit my lip, wondering if this was going to undo everything we had just managed to put back together again.

Pen nodded. "I think that would help immensely."

Lyall thought for a moment. "Sluag reckons even a Super Draugur won't be able to host a Dion permanently."

Pen nodded. "Yes, but Sluag has no reason to tell us the truth, and he has no experience of trying to put the soul of a Dion in to a Super."

I had to smile at Pen's use of our shortened name for the Super Draugur. She was the coolest old lady ever.

Lyall surprised me by what he said next. "I think we need to try it. The more Dion we have, the better."

Artair nodded. "I agree, and if it works, then Finlay gets to stick around permanently."

I smiled in gratitude. Artair had become a lot more forgiving since he had found Enid. Looking to Pen, I said, "I guess that settles it, then."

"When should we try?" Freya asked.

Pen looked to me and then Lyall. "I think Finlay needs to be asked if he is willing to participate first. Flora, you're the best person to speak to him."

I sneaked a sideways glance at Lyall, and he nodded encouragingly. "It should be you, love."

I stood. "Okay, I'll go and see him now."

Pen smiled at me. "Perfect. Once Finlay agrees, we can take the Super to the Everwood and try to switch the souls."

I leaned down and placed a kiss against Lyall's cheek before whispering, "Thank you, for being so understanding."

He grabbed my hand and squeezed it, murmuring, "Anything for you, love."

My heart was as light as my steps as I skipped down the stone stairs of the castle and in to the gardens. I eased into the Everwood with a liquid smoothness and inhaled deeply, delighted to be here, as always.

It was almost as though Finlay was expecting me. The little white light danced through the air and came to rest upon my shoulder.

Hi, Flor. You look in a seriously good mood tonight.

"I am but whether I stay in a good mood kind of depends on you," I admitted.

What do you need? His voice was half curious and half suspicious.

I took a deep breath and told him everything Pen had suggested. I tried to make it sound as positive as possible. I knew how Finlay felt about being in the body of a Draugur. Truthfully, I had no idea how he was going to react.

The little light went quiet and dimmed ever so slightly as I finished speaking, and I knew he was considering everything I had said. Finally, after what felt like forever, he spoke inside my mind.

I hate being like this. The last eight months have taught me that having any body is better than having none.

I couldn't hide my delight. "You want to do it? Really?"

I do. I want to be a person again, Flor.

I started to fade from the Everwood. There was no point in waiting. The sooner we got Finlay into pet's body, the sooner we could focus on kicking Sluag's ass.

Wait, Flor?

His serious tone stopped me dead, and I looked at him expectantly.

You know this is the last opportunity for me, don't you? If this doesn't work, then there's nothing else to try. Once everything is finished—once Sluag is defeated—I have to go, for good.

I blinked back tears as I nodded. "I know," I whispered.

Don't be afraid, Flor. I'll always love you.

"I'll always love you too," I said as I faded from the Everwood.

This had to work, I wasn't sure I was going to be able to deal with the alternative.

CHAPTER
4

Pen wasted no time in getting everything ready when I told her Finlay had agreed to try to take up residence inside the Super Draugur's body. She quickly made her way to the Everwood so she could explain to my best friend what he needed to do.

Lyall and I were tasked with fetching the Super Draugur from the cellars.

We approached the monster's cell cautiously. Manacles dangled from Lyall's hand, and as they clinked together, the Super eyed us both warily.

"What do you want Soul Keeper?" it hissed as it rose from where it had been slumped in the corner of its prison.

"Your time in that body is up. We're giving it to someone who deserves it," Lyall growled as he unlocked the door.

The Super Draugur shifted from one foot to the other as though it were considering how much of a fight it should put up. I was tense as Lyall approached it with the cuffs held ready.

"Lyall, be careful," I warned.

The creature spat in my general direction. "It's not him I want. It's you, Soul Keeper."

"You don't get to lay a finger on her, freak." Lyall rushed forward with supernatural speed and snapped the manacles on the Super Draugur's wrists.

I fired a smirk at the Super Draugur and stepped aside to allow Lyall to walk it out of the cell.

The Super hissed as it passed me. "Smile all you like, Flora. You won't feel so safe when Sluag opens up this one's throat and bleeds him like a pig."

Lyall didn't falter; instead, he kicked the Draugur in the back of its ankles and carried on walking it out of the cell.

I followed quietly after them, contemplating what the Super had said. I knew Lyall's death was the one thing that Sluag desired above anything else. It had occurred to me he would probably rather kill Lyall than myself because he knew how much it would hurt me to lose him.

As the time ticked down until my twenty-first birthday, I grew more and more nervous about what Sluag would do next.

I caught up with Lyall and the Super before laying my hand on its arm. As we both faded to the Everwood, our joint force pulled the creature with us, and it blinked as it arrived in a realm that was supposed to be off-limits for it.

Pen was waiting patiently with the little white Finlay-light floating in the air beside her head.

Pen eyed the Draugur warily as she spoke. "Okay, Flora, you're going to be using a lot of energy here. You must rely on

Lyall to support you."

I met Lyall's eye and smiled warmly. "Of course."

Pen nodded. "Make sure you save enough energy to obliterate the soul afterward, Flora."

Before I could respond, the Super kicked out at Lyall and tried to pull away from his grasp.

"Nooo, you can't kill me," it howled.

Lyall yanked the monster back so it landed hard on the ground, and I pulled a short sword from my hip and trained it at the hollow in the base of its throat.

"You can keep still and be quiet, or we can stop you from being able to try and run before we start," I growled.

The Super quieted down to low mumbles below its breath. I was pretty sure I heard it say something about death to every Dion, but I ignored it, instead turning to Lyall and holding out my hand to him.

"Ready?"

He took my hand and gave it a light squeeze. "Sure am."

I turned my gaze to the little white orb. "Finlay?"

Ready, Flor. He spoke inside my mind.

"Okay." I blew out a long, slow breath to steady my hammering heart, and I started to push with my energy.

I found the black pit inside the Super which was its rotten soul, and I allowed my energy to tease and wrap around it, pressing tighter and tighter all the time.

The Super started to wail with a high-pitched keening sound, and it rocked back and forth as it felt my power. I knew I needed to preserve some of my energy, and so I concentrated on the warmth of Lyall's hand entwined with mine.

He let out a soft gasp as he felt me tap in to his energy source and start to siphon it through myself and then into the body of the Super Draugur.

"Finlay," Pen beckoned to the waiting light. "Time for you to help out."

Finlay darted through the air obligingly and pressed himself firmly against the Super's chest. The Draugur hissed and thrashed violently as Finlay started to melt through the skin—just like the rogue soul had done on the CCTV screen all those months ago.

"That's it, keep going, all of you," Pen encouraged.

I redoubled my efforts and sent a wave of my own energy through the Draugur's body. I hadn't realised I had subconsciously demanded more of Lyall, and I was suddenly shocked as he staggered and groaned between clenched teeth.

Instinctually, I dropped his hand and tried to bear the burden entirely myself, but Lyall leaned forward and grabbed my hand, once again hissing, "I won't let you do this alone, love."

"It's hurting you," I ground out through clenched teeth.

We both concentrated on pushing even harder.

Suddenly, I felt a strange but familiar sensation as my energy snapped back into my body, almost sending me reeling backward. I heard a tiny "pop" as the Super Draugur's soul was forced out of the body, and I could sense a settling inside it as Finlay found his way into the newly vacated space.

The now homeless soul made a spiralling loop through the air before hurtling toward Lyall, who was currently kneeling on the ground gasping.

Without thinking, I hurled the words toward the soul that would obliterate it from this world. As I spoke, I hoped and prayed that this would work on a Super Draugur soul.

It did; the soul disappeared from sight in a flurry of curses and threats about the end of the world.

I dropped to my knees beside Lyall and tried desperately to stem the flow of rich, crimson blood that poured from my nose and onto my pale green top.

"Flora, are you all right?" Lyall reached out to touch my cheek. He was white and haggard-looking, and it terrified me.

I nodded I was okay before turning toward the body of the Super Draugur. It lay on its back with its eyes closed, and it had returned to its human form.

Pressing one hand to my nose, I desperately tried to stem the blood flow. I reached out tentatively with my other hand and touched the hand of the Super Draugur.

"Finlay? Are you in there?"

A moment of silence passed, before he blinked his eyes open and looked me directly in the eyes.

"That never fails to feel hideous. Flor, are you okay? You don't look great."

I smiled in relief, glad to know we had managed to find a way to put Finlay back into a body again. Now I just had to hope that this body would be strong enough to house the soul of a

Dion.

With a grimace, Finlay looked down at his hands. "Jesus, I'm seriously ancient. How old am I?"

Pen frowned at him. "It's probably not ideal, Finlay. It will do for now, though."

"If it works out in this body, I swear we'll find you a younger model and move you," I promised.

He turned unfamiliar eyes on me and smiled through the face of a man who must have been around forty. "I'll hold you to that, Flor."

Lyall was standing now, and he clapped a hand on Finlay's shoulder. "Good to have you back, mate. Now can we head back to the castle because I feel pretty rough."

A wave of dismay rushed through me as I took in how terrible Lyall looked. I took his hand in mine, catching his attention. "I'm not using you for energy anymore. It does you too much harm."

He gave me a pained half-smile. "You might have to when it comes down to facing off against Sluag, love."

I knew what he said was likely true, but I had to hope I wouldn't ever need to do this to Lyall again.

CHAPTER 5

Freya was at the gate, and she beamed at the new version of Finlay as we all approached the castle. She opened her arms and offered him a warm hug, which he accepted readily.

"Welcome back, again. Think you might manage to stick around for the full fight this time?" she quipped sarcastically.

Finlay laughed and released her from his hug before nodding his head to Bear.

"If I'd known you were into the older fellas I wouldn't have wasted my time, hotness," Bear joked.

Freya rolled her eyes. "Feel free to stop wasting your time right now."

Unperturbed, he waggled his eyebrows and laughed. "I'm in no rush. I know you want me."

"Urgh," was Freya's reply before she flounced off and disappeared into the castle.

"We need to start talking tactics." Pen looked pale and was absently pressing her hand to her forehead as she spoke.

"Are you all right, Pen?" Finlay gave the senior Dion a concerned stare.

She waved him away. "I'm fine, just a little tired right now. We should begin planning our next move now we have a full complement of Dion together."

"Shall we go to the hall?" I asked.

"I'll go and get everyone else," Lyall offered.

I grabbed hold of his hand before he left and shot him a questioning look. "Are you really okay?"

He gave me a wan smile. "I feel like death but I'll be okay, love."

I nodded and let him go before turning to Pen and studying her face. Her lips were pursed, and her eyes had a glassy sheen to them, almost as though she was trying to suppress a nagging pain.

Pen, Finlay, and I made our way to the great hall and sat in our usual places. Pen started to let her head drop to her hands but then seemed to think better of it—instead sitting rigidly straight and staring forward.

Leah was the first to arrive. She smiled at me before frowning at Pen and starting to speak, but Pen cut her off with a swift wave of the hand.

I narrowed my eyes but bit my tongue, deciding I would corner Pen once everyone had left the hall.

Lyall walked back in, and I was relieved to see he looked a lot better than when he had left. He was followed by Freya and Bear, and just after them, Artair and Enid.

I took a moment to appreciate my circle of Dion. I felt a warm and fuzzy rush of gratitude to know I had these people surrounding me and helping me to fight against the end of the mortal world.

"Thank you all for coming. Especially you, Finlay. I know how hard it must be to have to start over in another new body." Pen gave my best friend a warm smile as she spoke.

"Now that we're at full strength, we need to put a plan of attack together. We have to stop Sluag before this goes any further," Artair growled.

"Agreed," said Pen.

"I did have one suggestion." Enid had come a long way in the months following her failed kidnap attempt by Sluag's Draugur. She was now a highly proficient warrior and had built a beautiful relationship with the animal souls of the Everwood.

"Go ahead, Enid," Pen encouraged.

"We know that Flora can't kill all of the Draugur without harming herself. So, could we not try and get them to consume her blood so that they come over to our side?"

Artair smiled at her warmly. "Create an army who are loyal to Flora, using Sluag's Draugur. That's gonna make him seriously angry. I love it."

In principle it sounded like a great idea. "How will we get the blood into the Draugur though?" I asked.

There was a moment of silence as we all contemplated our own individual ways of getting the blood into Sluag's monsters.

"Do they have to drink? I mean like water, to stay alive?"

Freya asked.

Pen looked even paler than she had before. "Yes, they need to maintain the human body that houses their soul, so they will have to drink at some point or another."

"Well the only place I can think of for them to drink from in the Endwood is the river. If we get some of Flora's blood in there, we can get them all in one go," Freya grinned.

"Clever." Bear was smiling at Freya like a love-sick puppy.

Finlay tapped his chin thoughtfully. "That would mean sending someone to the Endwood with Flora's blood."

"That's too risky for any of you." I spoke quickly knowing that Sluag would move mountains to get hold of another Dion in the Endwood.

"Flora's right. If Sluag gets wind of another Dion in the Endwood, he will do anything to get hold of your blood for more Super Draugur," Leah agreed.

"It's too good an opportunity to miss. If we can convert all of the ordinary Draugur, then that only leaves us with the Supers and Sluag to deal with." Artair spoke determinedly.

I took a deep breath as I made my decision. "I'll do it myself."

"Not a bloody chance, love," Lyall growled.

I shook my head at him. "Hear me out first."

I was met with sceptical glares from my protectors, but I carried on regardless. "I can choose to go to the Endwood in my dream-form, and he can't hurt me then. I can still get my blood into the river, but Sluag won't be able to touch me."

Finlay looked worried. "He can still hurt you mentally, though, Flor. He's had eight months to save up all of the stuff he wants to torment you with."

"But, nobody will have to risk their lives if I go. It has to be me." My voice was firm.

"I think Flora is right," Pen spoke firmly. "This is the least risky option. Apart from not wanting to lose any of you, we can't afford to give Sluag a new blood supply for more Supers that we have no idea how to kill."

"Then it's decided. I'll go tonight," I said firmly.

Lyall shook his head angrily. "I won't leave your side while you're there."

I nodded. "Okay."

"So, we're going to have an army to help shield us from Sluag, but that still doesn't help us to kill his Super Draugur," Bear said what we were all thinking.

"I'm confident the best way to stop the Super Draugur is to kill Sluag." Pen spoke slowly, and I could tell she was feeling even worse than before.

I felt a flicker of guilt as I remembered back to my conversation with Sluag.

I am not their true maker. That honour belongs to the traitor whose blood was used in their creation.

I hadn't told anyone else that the Supers could supposedly be killed if Finlay was killed. How could I? Betraying the one person who had always been there for me wasn't an option.

Yet, as the likelihood of one or more of my Dion being killed in this war increased, so did my guilt at keeping my secret.

"But we don't know if we can kill him," Enid said.

"I'm investigating the possibility of dislodging his soul, in much the same way the rogues have done in the mortal world," Pen replied.

"Sluag has a soul?" I squeaked in surprise.

"Sluag was a man before he was the Host of the Unforgiven Dead, Flora. Of course, he has a soul. It is twisted and black and rotten, but a soul nonetheless," Pen confirmed.

Wow, who knew?

"So, we can dislodge his soul, and he'll be gone for good?" Artair asked.

"Put simply, yes. The problem is, I don't think Flora has the power to do it, even with Lyall as back-up," Pen admitted.

I shuddered as I thought of draining Lyall to try to kick Sluag's soul out of his body.

"So, it can't be done?" Leah asked quietly.

Pen rubbed her eyes with the palm of her hand. "I think it can, but I just don't think we know how yet. I will keep working on it."

"Pen, I think you need some rest." Finlay stood and hooked his arm through hers.

"I think you're right. I'm sorry, I must be coming down with something." Pen allowed Finlay to help her up and walk her to the door.

"I'll go to the Endwood tonight. Hopefully we can at least start to recruit Draugur to our side soon." I stood up and Lyall followed suit.

"Thank you, Flora, and please be careful," Pen warned before she allowed Finlay to lead her from the room.

"I meant what I said, love. I'm not leaving you alone while you're there," Lyall murmured to me.

I nodded in agreement, glad I would have him by my side. Truth be told, I wasn't thrilled at the thought of possibly running into Sluag after all this time.

CHAPTER
6

Lyall kicked off his boots and sat comfortably on my bed. He patted the covers beside him, and I quickly followed suit—kicking my own boots off and stretching out next to him. I laid my head on his thigh, and he stroked my hair softly, helping me to relax.

"I'm worried about Pen," I murmured.

His hand hesitated for a fraction of a second before continuing to caress my hair.

"So am I. Finlay's with her right now. She'll be all right, love. We just need to concentrate on getting you in and out of the Endwood before Sluag notices."

"Not very likely," I admitted sleepily.

"Shhh, love. Let's get this done so I know I have you back safely," he whispered.

As I started to drift off to sleep, I thought of the charred trees and blackened grass of the Endwood. Imagining the scene surrounding me in the same way I would imagine the Everwood to take myself there.

I felt myself slipping further and further into oblivion, until with a gentle jolt I was there, in the domain of my enemy.

I turned my head left and then right, wondering which direction would lead me to the river quicker. Making my decision, I turned left and began to jog through the trees.

There was a constant creeping cold that wound its way through the air of the Endwood, which was made even more stark and unpleasant by the muted light of the moon. I shivered as I pressed on through the trees.

A sudden sound caused me to hurl myself against the nearest tree, hiding my body from the path I had been following. My heart hammered in my chest as I watched two Supers stroll along the way I had just walked.

They behaved as though they had always been here, and it sent ice down my spine.

As soon as the Supers were out of sight I slipped around the tree trunk and carried on through the trees. After a couple more minutes of tense jogging, I stopped as my ears picked up the sound of running water.

I smiled to myself, delighted I had chosen the right path to the river. I headed in the direction of the babbling sound and quickly came out of the trees and onto a riverbank.

The water was black, as I had expected, and it swirled in little eddies as it passed where I stood. I stared into the depths for a moment, mesmerised by the rhythmic pulse of the miniature whirlpools sweeping by.

A gasp escaped me as a bony, white face appeared through the inky darkness. It was a koi carp, but it was just the skeleton of the fish that swam through the water. Its ivory-coloured bones a stark contrast to the pitch-black water, and its mouth opening and closing as though pulling water through non-existent gills.

"Well, that's not at all disturbing," I murmured to myself as I pulled a small, silver knife from my pocket and turned my left hand over to expose my palm.

I sighed as I took in the raised and bumpy scar tissue that stretched across the skin. I had cut my hand so many times since becoming the Soul Keeper, that it was a complete mess now, and here I was about to do it again.

I wasn't sure how much blood would be enough, since it would be diluted by the water, so I pushed the point of the knife deep into my hand and then dragged it through my palm, creating a deep trench that immediately filled with crimson.

"Ouch."

I stepped forward and turned my hand over to allow my blood to run into the water, massaging the skin around the wound to encourage the sticky liquid to flow harder.

After around five minutes, I figured I had probably let about a pint of my blood leak into the water. I didn't really have much more to spare so I guessed it would have to be enough. I tore a strip of cloth from my T-shirt and wrapped my hand tightly to stem the bleeding.

Turning my back on the river, I started to walk back toward the tree line and began to imagine my bedroom back at Castle

Dion.

"Hello, Little Dreamer," Sluag hissed from behind me.

Ahh Shit!

I desperately tried to get a firm grip on the image of my room, but the surprise of running into Sluag knocked my concentration.

I whirled around to face him. "I'm not planning on stopping, Sluag. Just a flying visit."

He grinned, exposing his yellowed teeth. "I must say, I am surprised to see you here voluntarily, Flora. May I ask why you are in my Endwood?"

I knew it was a huge mistake to get involved in any sort of conversation with him, but I couldn't help but wonder if I might be able to get any more information about his Super Draugur.

"I just thought I'd stop by and see how your little project was going?" I tried to sound casual.

He laughed caustically, and the sound made my blood run cold.

"You mean since you murdered my colleague?" He raised one sparse eyebrow as he spoke.

Every time I thought about what I had done to Lyall's mother, I felt sick. I was sure I'd never be able to dull the image of her torn open throat from my mind.

"Well, you must be struggling to create Supers without help in the mortal world." I sounded calmer than I felt.

"Oh, Little Dreamer, have you not realised that I have more help than I could possibly dream of in the mortal world now that

I have so many rogue souls placed in their new bodies."

Of course, he didn't need a regular human when he had hundreds of hi-jacked people to do his bidding for him.

"So, you must've run out of Dion blood by now then?" I queried.

"I have. Are you here to offer me some more?" Grinning, he took a step closer.

"You've had all you're going to get, Sluag," I growled as I took a step back.

"I must say, I'm a little surprised, Flora. I would have thought a ruthless killer such as yourself, would have accepted that you need to obliterate Finlay's soul in order to destroy my Super Draugur by now."

"That's never going to happen," I ground out.

He narrowed his eyes at me. "Lyall agrees with you, does he?"

"Don't bring him in to this, Sluag," I hissed. It was time for me to get the hell out of there.

"You haven't told him, have you? Is that because you know he'd have Finlay marked for death before you had a chance to say, 'sorry I killed your mother'?" Sluag smirked.

I curled my lip in disgust. "Jesus, you're disgusting, aren't you? I found out today that you were a man once. What happened to make you so completely ruined, Sluag?"

He studied me quietly for a moment before he answered me. "Betrayal does strange things to everyone, Little Dreamer."

I had been about to make a break for the safety of my room

again, but the tone of his voice made me genuinely curious. "Who betrayed you?"

"That is of little consequence after thousands of years, Flora. Why don't you just give Lyall to me. You know I'm going to get a hold of him eventually anyway?"

"Ha, don't be ridiculous. I would burn before I gave him to you, Sluag," I snarled.

"But will you let the world burn, before you admit you need to obliterate Finlay's soul, Little Dreamer? I think that's the bigger question, right now," he taunted.

The time for getting information about Sluag's Supers was over. I was only going to get hurt if I stayed here any longer.

"As thrilling as our little chats are, I think it's time for me to go, Sluag." I started to fade from his view as I forced myself to concentrate on going back to the arms of the man who was watching over me in the mortal world.

Sluag looked at me with real pity. "I think you might be back sooner than you think, Little Dreamer. Don't underestimate the importance of blood."

I had no idea what he meant. Did he know what I had done with my blood?

Too late, the Endwood faded from my sight, and I woke to find Lyall's concerned amber eyes burning into my own through the darkness.

"Good to have you back, love. Did you get it done?" Lyall pulled me against him and kissed the top of my head.

"I did, although I ran into Sluag while I was there." I

frowned.

Lyall's grip on me tightened ever so slightly. "What did he say?"

I shrugged. "Not much, actually. He's out of Finlay's blood."

"Good," he replied brightly.

"Now that he has rogue souls in the mortal world, he has people to help him create more Super Draugur," I confessed.

Lyall sighed. "So, he's gonna want more Dion blood?"

"Yep." I wrapped my arms around Lyall and held on to him tightly, as though Sluag couldn't hurt him if I did.

"Then we need to make sure that we keep security tight, love. He's not getting hold of another one of us."

"Agreed," I murmured.

"For now, let's try and get some sleep. We can tell the others everything in the morning."

I didn't need telling twice. I burrowed into him, and I was asleep within seconds.

CHAPTER
7

"Flora."

I was warm and cosy, and I had been safe in Lyall's arms when I fell asleep. *So why did his voice sound so worried and urgent?*

"Flora, wake up, love," Lyall hissed in my ear.

My eyes snapped open and instantly locked with Lyall's. His amber wolf-eyes were wide with worry, and he pressed a finger to his lips, indicating I be quiet.

The noises reached my ears then. I could hear banging and shouting ringing through the castle. Terrified, I swung my legs over the edge of the bed and tried to run for the door.

Lyall stood and grabbed my wrist before pulling me backward, until I was pressed against his chest and his mouth was tickling my ear.

"We're under attack, love, and I have no clue how many are out there," he whispered.

"The others," I whimpered.

"We'll do what we can, Flora, but I have to get you out of here. You have to promise to stay by my side and let me protect you."

I started to argue that we needed to help the others.

He cut me off with a growl. "Non-negotiable, love. We'll see what we can do once we know what we're fighting against."

I blinked and then nodded once. "Okay."

We approached my bedroom door, with Lyall leading the way. It was still dark outside, and the hallway was shadowy as we opened the wooden door and stepped through.

A noise on the lower floor made us both lean over the bannister to stare at three Super Draugur, who were systematically working their way through the rooms downstairs—obviously looking for us.

Suddenly, my heart jumped as two figures emerged from the shadows on our right. Lyall pulled his sword and stepped in front of me before I realised it was Enid and Artair. I swore under my breath with relief.

"What's happening?" Artair whispered.

"I'm guessing Sluag got tired of waiting to get his claws into a new Dion," Lyall hissed.

Enid jumped at a loud crash as she spoke. "We need to get out of here."

We started to make our way to the staircase, trying to keep hidden by the shadows wherever possible.

"What about Finlay and Pen?" I stopped walking.

"Flora, let me get you out, and I swear I'll come back in to find them?" Lyall practically begged.

I allowed him to grab my hand and tug me down the stairs behind him. I gasped in shock to see there were more Supers kicking in the doors of the downstairs rooms.

"There must be at least twenty Supers here." Artair's face was deathly white as he realised how dire our predicament was.

"Just keep to the shadows and follow me," Lyall instructed.

We hesitated a moment until the main hallway seemed clear, before breaking into a headlong run toward the front gate.

When we arrived at the gate, I was shocked to find it standing wide open. It was always locked at night to prevent surprise attacks.

Lyall frowned as he took in the wide-open gate.

"Someone betrayed us from the inside." Artair said out loud what we were all thinking.

A sound behind us alerted us to the approach of two Super Draugur, and there was no more time to wonder who the traitor was.

"Run," shouted Enid.

We bolted into the castle gardens and toward Loch Ness.

"The boat," Artair yelled across the night air.

"Let's just hope they can't swim," Lyall growled as we headed to the tiny boat that had first brought me to Castle Dion almost a year ago.

My heart hurt as I thought of Finlay at the helm of the boat, and I turned back as though I might see him escaping the castle behind us.

A rough hand grabbed my arm and dragged me down the bank to the loch. "There's no time for that, Flora. We need to get you out of here."

Artair pulled me to the boat and practically threw me on board next to Enid. Lyall was standing on the shore waiting to push the boat off into the water.

Artair followed me into the boat, and Lyall started to untie the ropes. The two Supers were visible at the top of the hill now.

"Get them to the safehouse. I'll see you when I can," Lyall said to Artair.

Artair nodded his agreement, but I stood up in blind panic.

"What do you mean? You're not coming with us?" My voice was high-pitched.

"I need to go back and get the others. Artair will keep you safe until I catch up with you." Lyall finished untethering the boat and started to push it away from the shore.

"Lyall, don't leave me, please?" My voice was small now, and tears burned my eyes.

"I won't be gone long, love. You'll never forgive me if I don't help Pen and Finlay out." He touched a gentle hand to my cheek before the boat floated too far from the shore.

Leaning toward him, I pressed my lips against his and kissed him fiercely. "You better find us soon," I whispered.

"I promise," he whispered before pulling back from me and diving into the shadows of the trees just in time to avoid the two approaching Supers.

The Draugur stood on the shore and howled at us as we

disappeared across the loch. Clearly, they weren't up for a swim, and I was thankful for their aversion to water as we slowly drifted farther and farther out of their reach.

I sat in shock, staring at the stand of trees Lyall had just disappeared into when suddenly the upper floors of the castle illuminated with a blaze of orange light.

"It's on fire," I gasped.

Enid laid a gentle hand on my shoulder. "It's going to be okay, Flora. They'll all make it out."

Every part of me wanted to begin rowing back to land. I looked at the oars, which were now in Artair's hands as he steered us toward the far shore, but he shook his head at me.

"Not going to happen, Flora. I'm more afraid of what Lyall will do to me than you."

I turned back to watch the fire take full hold of the place I had called home for months now, and I realised that we weren't going to be able to go back.

My eyes reflected the flames that licked at the night sky, and the tears that rolled down my cheeks were tinged with fire.

"Where will we go?" I asked brokenly.

"There's a place that Pen has kept secret. It's our safe-haven if ever something like this happens." Artair kept his face emotionless as he spoke, but I could hear the desolation in his voice.

"How did I never know about it?" My voice was shaky.

"Because you never needed to. You will always have at least one Dion with you in these kinds of circumstances."

"Is it far away from here?" I asked, wondering how long it would take for the others to arrive.

"No, it's not far. It's nothing like the castle, Flora. It's a pretty miserable place, but that's why Pen chose it. It's unlikely Sluag will search for us there." Artair grunted at the effort of rowing.

I turned away from the inferno which now engulfed the castle. I couldn't look at it any longer, and I fell silent until we reached the far shore of Loch Ness.

Eventually, the tiny boat bounced off land, and all three of us jumped out onto the bank.

"Come on, it's not too far to go." Artair spoke gently, sensing how fragile my emotions were right now.

We set off up the bank and into a densely wooded forest with Artair leading the way. We had no torches for light, so progress was slow as we stumbled blindly through the woods.

We walked in silence for over an hour before the landscape changed. The trees thinned out, and the terrain became increasingly rocky. I was surprised to step out of the tree line and suddenly find myself standing on a railway line.

I jumped back in panic, afraid I had escaped the Super Draugur only to end up getting flattened by a train.

Artair almost smiled. "Don't worry, the line's disused. We'll follow the tracks from here to where we're going."

I had no energy left to question where we were going; instead, Enid and I fell into step behind him, walking carefully between the rusty tracks.

After an age, we reached a square, single-storey building that hunkered at the foot of a hill. The tracks we followed flowed to two huge front doors that were covered over with nailed-in boards before disappearing inside.

The building was derelict, with boards covering all of the windows and barely any paint left on the exterior walls.

Artair didn't hesitate. He walked to one of the boarded windows and wrestled the wood away.

"What is this place?" Enid's eyes were wide.

"It used to be a rail terminal, but it hasn't been used in decades. So, now it's our safehouse."

We stepped inside, and Artair flicked a switch that fired up a few dim lights in the roof.

It was dark, depressing, and uncared for—the perfect place to lie low and stay undiscovered.

"Sorry it's not what you're used to," Artair said apologetically.

I looked around at the damp walls, peeling plaster, and the tiny, dirty kitchen area before taking a deep breath. "We're alive, that's what matters. What now?"

"Now we wait for the others," he said grimly.

CHAPTER 8

It turned out the ceiling lights were battery powered, but there was a generator that would supply power to the building once it was switched on. Artair headed to the basement to get us up and running.

"Don't leave her side," he murmured to Enid, touching his fingers to hers in a brief moment of tenderness before he started down the steps to the dark underbelly of the terminal.

I shuddered, glad it wasn't me going down into the pitch darkness.

I suddenly heard a thunderous thrumming sound, and for a few moments I panicked, not knowing what the hell it was. Enid was checking out the small kitchen area, and she jumped and raised her head too.

We both relaxed simultaneously as we realised the sound was coming from a downpour of rain on the corrugated tin roof which sat atop the building—it was going to take a while to become familiar with the sounds here.

I crossed the bare earthen floor to a battered, wooden door and unlocked it before yanking it back on squealing hinges. I flinched.

"Undercover, Flora," Enid reprimanded.

"Sorry," I murmured as I rested my shoulder against the doorframe and stared out into the bleak night.

Three of us were safely here, but six of us were still out there in the inhospitable darkness. My Dion would be cold, wet, and afraid. *Were they all still okay? Had I lost anyone?*

I sucked in a deep breath, my lungs filling with cold, damp air, and I wrapped my arms around myself. I dug my nails into the tender flesh of my upper arms, using the pinching feeling to keep me grounded when all I wanted to do was run out into the night and try to find them.

"Get your ass here, Lyall," I whispered under my breath.

A sudden sound from somewhere in the trees surrounding the terminal sent me reaching for the short sword that hung at my hip. I held my breath and stared into the darkness, waiting for a Draugur or Super to appear.

When Freya's tall form stepped out from the tree cover, I blew out the breath I had been holding and quickly crossed the front yard of the building to meet her.

When Finlay and Bear emerged behind her—supporting an extremely sick-looking Pen between them—I whimpered in relief.

I passed Freya, and we gave each other a warm hug before she continued toward the muted light that trickled from the open door.

I reached the others, and my eyes widened when I saw exactly how sick Pen was. "Are you all right?" I whispered.

Finlay's face was dark as he practically carried Pen with Bear's help. "We need to get her inside and warm. Something's wrong, Flora. She doesn't just have the flu."

I walked beside them in silence, already soaked through and shivering from the rain.

Once we were inside, Finlay and Bear gently laid Pen down on a dusty sofa bed, and Freya covered her with a rough woollen blanket. Pen was barely conscious by now.

I beckoned Finlay to a corner of the room, and he gave me a hug. "I'm so glad you're safe, Flor."

"Me too, but Pen's not safe, Finlay. She needs a hospital and quickly." I stared into his once again unfamiliar eyes.

The pain in his eyes hurt my heart. "If we take her to a hospital, she'll be a sitting duck for Sluag, Flor. He'll kill her."

"If we don't take her, I'm pretty sure the outcome will be the same. She *needs* professional help, Finlay," I argued.

"If we take her to the hospital, I can't leave her alone. I have to stay with her and guard her. That means I can't take care of you." He was torn.

"That's okay. I have the other Dion to look out for me here." I looked over at the others. They were switching heaters on in the main room and the smaller rooms that would likely serve as bedrooms, now that Artair had kicked the generator into life.

My eyes flickered back to study Finlay's face. "Did you see

him? He went back to find you."

He knew I meant Lyall. He was silent for a moment before he answered me. "We didn't see him, or Leah. I figured he came with you, to protect you on the way to the safehouse."

I could tell by his face he was telling me the truth. I'd known Finlay long enough to be able to pick apart any lies he told.

"No news is good news, right?" I tried to sound upbeat, but inside I felt as though my heart was breaking apart. I couldn't live without Lyall.

Finlay pulled me in to a bear hug. "He'll be here, Flor. He wouldn't leave you to face Sluag alone. He's too damn stubborn for that."

A wracking cough from across the room brought our attention back to Pen. Freya was standing over our oldest Dion, stroking Pen's silver hair and murmuring comforting words.

"She needs a hospital." Artair's voice said he wasn't compromising, and I agreed.

"She does. Finlay has said he will take her and stay with her." I nodded to my best friend.

"I'll get the car from the garage." Artair wasted no time in disappearing through the still open door.

"Keep your phone switched on and check in with us every two hours, okay?" Freya spoke firmly.

Finlay nodded before looking toward me. "Don't let anything happen to her."

"You know we won't." Enid's voice was low and determined.

Once again, I marvelled at how far she had come since she first met Lyall and me. My stomach clenched as I thought of my wolf-eyed Dion. He was out there somewhere, and I should have been looking for him. It's what he would do for me. But I had no idea where to start; he could have been anywhere.

Finlay leaned over Pen and gently lifted her from the sofa. He crossed the room to the front door and moved quickly through the rain to lay Pen's prone body across the back seat of the car, and then fixed the blanket around her cold body.

Artair handed the keys to Finlay, and they both nodded to each other. I felt a brief flicker of relief at Artair's seeming forgiveness of Finlay after all this time.

Finlay slid into the driver's seat and started to ease the car through the trees, the lights of the car fading into the squalling rain showers until we were left in just the sickly yellow glow of the terminal lights once more.

"We should get some sleep." Even after everything that had happened, Bear was still his usual upbeat self. "We'll be warmer if we share a bed." This last was directed at Freya.

"I'd rather freeze," she huffed before stalking to one of the small rooms at the back of the building that were furnished with thin mattresses and slamming the door behind her.

Bear sheepishly chose another room and nodded goodnight to us before closing the door behind him.

Artair and Enid started toward their own rooms. "You should get some sleep, Flora," Artair said softly.

I had moved to one of the windows. I could barely see

anything through the rivers of rain that poured down the glass, but I settled myself into a threadbare chair and pulled a thin blanket around my shoulders.

"I can't, Artair. Not until I know he's safe," I whispered.

He started to speak again, but Enid laid a gentle hand on his chest and shook her head at him.

"Okay." He nodded once before they both headed to bed, leaving me alone in my silent vigil.

CHAPTER 9

Finlay was true to his word, and after two hours, my phone beeped to let me know I had a text. I tore my eyes from the view out the window for long enough to read the words on the screen, and my heart sank.

We're at the hospital, Flor. They're doing tests. It doesn't look good. F x

My chest tightened as I read the simple sentences. I bit my lip as I typed my reply and hit send.

What's wrong with her? Do you know yet? F x

I returned my gaze to the window. The rain was relentless. It hadn't even slowed a tiny bit. My eyes followed the raindrop rivers as they raced down the glass, hurrying to join their comrades in the flow of water that ran over the cracked and split wood of the exterior window sill.

My phone beeped again, and I fought the urge to hit the power off button. If Pen was really and truly ill, I didn't want to know.

They suspect it's a brain aneurysm!

No kiss, no "F," just the cold, hard facts. I bit down on a sob, not wanting to wake the others. Pen had always been like a mother to me and Finlay. The thought of not having her around hurt too much.

Can they help her Finlay?

His reply came too quickly.

I don't think they can, Flor!

I started to write a response but deleted it after a few words. I tried several more times over the next few minutes to think of the right thing to say. I knew Finlay would be a wreck right now, and he was alone in the hospital, dealing with everything. The words just wouldn't come, though.

My phone beeped again, and I quickly drank in the words on the screen.

There's one thing that would cure her.

Immortal blood. I read about it in one of the manuscripts. Immortal blood will heal any illness, a bit like in stories about vampires, Flor.

I reread the text three times. At first, I thought he meant my blood because my soul was immortal, but I quickly realised that what he actually meant was the Host of the Unforgiven Dead's blood. Both Sluag's body and soul were immortal. He was unique. That must have been what Sluag meant when he told me I would be back sooner than I thought.

I felt a flicker of anger and desperation as I replied.

Yeah, okay, I'll just call down to the Endwood and ask Sluag to lend me some blood. Not likely, Finlay.

I let my head drop to my hands and growled aloud. The one thing that might help Pen was the one thing I couldn't do. Nothing on earth would make Sluag give me his blood.

After another ten minutes had passed, I realised Finlay wasn't going to reply. Why would he? I figured he had more important things to focus on.

After another five minutes of complete indecision, I stood up and let the blanket fall back onto the chair. Crossing the room to the door, I slipped quietly out into the rain, and I imagined the Everwood around me.

I quickly appeared amongst the blue-flowered trees, and I

wasn't really surprised to see a few random snowflakes falling from the sky. One settled against my hair before quickly melting in the warmth of my body.

"Well at least I know I've definitely been betrayed," I murmured, wondering once again who had left the gate to Castle Dion open.

I began to make my way through the Everwood, and as I walked I felt a sense of relief. If I truly had been betrayed, then the prophecy had been fulfilled. I was no longer fated to die before my twenty-first birthday.

Pure souls bobbed through the trees, dipping and spinning through the air. They celebrated my presence as though I were a god, and I guessed in a strange way, I was their god.

I barely had to even try to imagine the silver threads that would connect our souls and let me speak to them all at once. With a mental flourish, I sent around three hundred souls skittering off delightedly through the trees.

A rogue bobbed toward me, and I obliterated it without hesitation.

I was a Soul Keeper, and I was finally quite good at it. I felt my confidence rise a little as I approached the boundary line between my beautiful land and Sluag's Endwood.

I could have tried to sleep so I could meet Sluag in the dream version of the Endwood, but my likelihood of sleeping when I was torn-up by thoughts of Lyall and Pen was zero. So, here I was for real.

Stopping before I reached the Endwood, I looked around

me. There was no sign of Sluag or any of his Draugur. I wasn't going to achieve anything without his presence, so I called out his name.

"Sluag?" It came out louder than I had intended, and I pressed my fingertips over my lips and shivered while I waited to see if he would come.

He sauntered through the blackened trees with a huge smile on his rotten face. "Flora, I can't keep you away these days."

I shrugged. "What can I say, I guess we're besties now."

He snorted. "No, not *besties*," he said the word like it tasted unpleasant to him. "But I do think we are coming to understand each other a little, don't you think?"

I thought about it for a moment before I replied. "You know, I think I'd understand you a lot better if I knew what happened before you became the Host of the Unforgiven Dead."

He tilted his head to one side as he studied my face. The scaly grey skin of his neck tightened, and his wisps of hair drooped under the gravity. His fire-pit eyes burned as he appeared to consider my proposal.

He finally seemed to reach a decision, and he slowly made his way to a pair of conveniently located tree stumps. One was on his side of the border and the other was on my side, but they faced each other with only a couple of metres separating them.

He sat down on his stump and gestured that I do the same on mine. There were none of the usual grand flourishes and theatrics I had become so used to from him.

I crossed to the tree stump, and after one final check that it was definitely all the way on my side of the border, I sat down and faced my enemy.

The silence between us stretched out into the realms of uncomfortable and I fought the urge to say something to fill it.

Finally, he spoke.

"I've never talked about my time before here with anyone. I would never have imagined to discuss it with a Soul Keeper. But, here we are."

I couldn't help but think he was trying to sound more untouched by his past than he really was. I stayed quiet and waited for him to begin.

"You already know I was one of the first men to walk on earth. I lived in a much simpler time than the one you do, Flora. Sometimes I envy the wonders today's humans have access to, and sometimes I pity you for how complex you make even the basic things in life.

"Anyway, I lived in a settlement, and we foraged and farmed to survive. In those times there was no real speech. We would communicate with sounds and gestures. We were animals, Flora. Just another part of the food chain.

But, although we may not have been able to actually say it, we were capable of feeling love and a desire to reproduce. So, I had a partner and a child."

CHAPTER 10

My mouth dropped open in surprise. I could no way imagine Sluag as a father and in love with a woman. Noting my disbelief, he continued.

"Humans are weak and susceptible to such feelings. I was no different. Now I am immortal, I am completely different, Little Dreamer.

"We lived not far from another settlement, and that meant fights over food and territory would often break out. I was involved in many of these skirmishes as I was a young male in my prime.

"One such fight began just outside our settlement one night, and the trouble spilled over to the huts we lived in. I knew I needed to get back to my family, and I fought my way there. It was slow progress and took me over half an hour. All the while I was afraid of what might have befallen them both."

Despite my hatred of Sluag, I found myself leaning forward eagerly. It was fascinating to hear about this other life of his.

He sounded distant now as he recounted the events that changed his life.

"When I finally got to our home, I found one of our own men inside. He was related to me in some way—a cousin, I think. When I arrived, he had just finished killing my family. Both of them had their heads dashed in, and they were laid out on the floor of the hut. There was no reason for doing what he did. I think perhaps, he may have been jealous of me."

I felt a twinge of sympathy for the Sluag who had been through the loss of his family, just like I had. But I quickly steeled myself against empathising with the immortal monster who now sat opposite me.

"Not long after those events, I became who I am now. The world quickly realised its mistake in the creation of humanity, and it desperately sought a way to control the demons that had been unleashed. I was one half of the resolution and you are the other, Little Dreamer."

"I'm sorry you were betrayed, and you lost your family." I said it with sincerity.

He stood quickly. "Ha. I don't need condolences, Flora. It was an event that happened so long ago, I cannot even recall their faces. I am immortal. I do not feel sadness, regret, or pain."

"Then why are you still so bitter that you have to destroy the world for every other human?" I spat.

"You don't see it the way I do, Little Dreamer. Humans have damaged this planet beyond repair, and they will continue to do so until there is nothing left. I don't see a reason to let them carry on."

I clenched my fists in frustration, a small part of me acknowledging he was a little bit right. "I've just given hundreds of souls another chance at existence. The reason I did that was because they were good and pure and kind. Not every human is twisted and broken like your rogues, Sluag."

He nodded at me silently. "Eternity is a very long time, Flora. I don't want to spend an hour longer than I have to, stuck here in the Endwood."

I thought about that. "Can't we work something out? A way for both of us to be happy?"

He smiled, his hideous mouth splitting apart to reveal his yellowed teeth. "Step over to this side of the border, Little Dreamer. I can use your blood to completely tear down the veil, and I will be free. That would make me happy."

"You know I won't do that, Sluag. Mainly because you can't be trusted once you escape the Endwood." I frowned.

"Then how can we ever reach a deal, Flora?" He leaned down until his face was as close to mine as it could be, without crossing the border.

"You said eternity was too long in the Endwood. If you help me, I can set you free. You don't have to stay here forever." I spoke with forced nonchalance.

A fleeting darkness momentarily crossed Sluag's face before he broke out into a yelping laughter that went on and on for what seemed like hours. He slapped his thigh in his mirth and threw back his head to guffaw at the sky.

He finally stopped laughing long enough to speak. "Oh, Flora Bast. Did you just offer to kill me and try to make it sound as though you were doing me a favour?"

I shrugged. "Forever is gonna get boring eventually, right?"

Still beaming, he sat back down on the tree stump opposite me and took a deep breath.

"Why are you really here, Flora?" His eyes locked onto mine, and I couldn't look away.

"I think you know why," I whispered.

"Penthesilea is dying, is she not?" His words were devoid of emotion.

I swallowed around the sob that threatened at the back of my throat. "Yes," I managed.

"Why, exactly did you come here, to see me?" He was going to drag this out and make it as painful as he possibly could.

"Because the only thing that can save her is the blood of an immortal and you're the only one I know." I met his gaze steadily, refusing to look away.

Tapping his long and bony fingers against his chin, Sluag appeared to seriously ponder my statement.

"Are you asking me to give you my blood, Little Dreamer?"

I nodded. "Yes."

"No." His reply came quickly.

"I'd hoped we could make a deal of some kind," I suggested.

He narrowed his eyes at me. "What could you possibly offer me, Flora?"

I shuffled forward, until I was perched on the edge of my

seat and I smiled at him. "I don't know. Do you have any suggestions?"

He grinned and his eyes burned. "I have one."

"Go on." I encouraged.

He moved forward until he was right at the edge of his own seat. Our faces were separated by only a few inches of air now.

"Give me Lyall?" He was as still as a statue as his fire-pit eyes glinted, so close I could see my own reflection in the centres.

"I can't." I mirrored him, unflinching as I stared back at his scaly face.

"Why?" he hissed.

I leaned forward a little more. I knew the tip of my nose was only a millimetre from the border now.

"I don't know where he is," I confessed quietly.

Seeming to enjoy the game, Sluag leaned closer to me. He was so close now, I could see his tufts of hair ruffling in the breeze from my short, sharp breaths.

"If you knew where he was, would you give him to me?" Sluag spoke so softly I almost didn't hear him.

This was my one chance. My hand had been hovering over my knife for the last few minutes. Now, I ripped it free from its sheath, and rearing back, I slashed the blade down through the air between us and sank it into Sluag's thigh.

"No, I wouldn't," I yelled as Sluag howled in fury.

I was acutely aware that I was on his side of the border, and as he grabbed at my arms, I threw myself backward, toppling my whole body over my tree stump and falling into an undignified backward roll.

A few strands of my hair had been wrapped around his spindly fingers, and fire ripped through my skull as the momentum parted the strands from my head.

"You bitch," Sluag roared as he smashed against the invisible barrier that prevented him from following me into the Everwood.

Sitting up, I assessed the blood that tipped my blade with a smile, and pushed it carefully back into its sheath. I looked over at my adversary, watching him rage up and down the line in the grass, shrieking obscenities at me.

I only hoped I had enough of his blood to heal Pen.

As though reading my mind, Sluag calmed and focussed his furious eyes on mine. "It's not enough to save her, Flora. She will still die."

I had to hope he was wrong. "We'll see, won't we."

I started to fade from sight, desperate to get back to the mortal world and get Sluag's blood to Pen.

His next words chilled me to the bone. "You have just destroyed any chance you might have had at mercy, Little Dreamer. When this veil is truly broken, I will annihilate everything you love before your very eyes, and then I will tear you asunder."

When I re-emerged before the railway terminal, I stood, trembling in the downpour for a moment until I was completely soaked to the bone, and my breathing had slowed down enough I could be sure I wouldn't pass out.

SOUL ETERNAL

CHAPTER 11

Realising—despite the sheath—I might lose some of the valuable blood from the blade of my knife if I stayed out in the rain any longer, I started toward the derelict building.

A sudden sound behind me made me swivel around and thrust the blade out in the general direction of the noise.

"Who's there?" I challenged.

A dark figure emerged from the trees and started toward me. I was just about to warn it to stop or I would attack, when it spoke.

"Not the welcome I was hoping for, love."

Without hesitation I launched into a headlong run and threw myself into his waiting arms.

"Lyall. Oh, my God, it's you, it's really you." I pressed my face against his chest and breathed in his scent as tears joined the rainwater on my cheeks.

He squeezed me tightly and then wrapped his arm around my shoulders, pulling me in the direction of the terminal.

"You're soaking, love. Let's get you indoors."

The sounds of my excitement at Lyall's return had disturbed the others, and they were all standing in the main room when we walked inside.

"Lyall, good to have you back." Artair smiled.

"You're both soaked. Flora, is that blood on your knife?" Enid asked questioningly as I drew my blade from its sheath.

"Um, yeah. I need to explain a few things, and then I really need to get to the hospital."

I recounted the events of the last hour, starting with Finlay's text and ending with Lyall's arrival.

Lyall frowned at me when I finished speaking. "I leave you alone for half a day, and you go and get into a full-on fight with Sluag. Flora, what the hell were you thinking?"

"That I needed to do something to help Pen." I spoke defensively.

"Any one of us could have gone to the Endwood to get Sluag's blood, Flora," Enid admonished.

I stood up. "I know, but I'm the only one who could get close enough to him to do it. Look, I'm cold and wet. I'm going to get a quick shower, and then I need to get this blade to Pen."

"I'll show you where the showers are," Artair offered.

"I'm coming with you to the hospital, love," Lyall insisted.

"Okay, give me fifteen minutes to get cleaned up." I followed Artair along a cold, narrow corridor that opened into a communal washroom which housed six shower cubicles.

"There's some shampoo and stuff on the shelf." Artair

pointed at a collection of bottles before he left me alone.

Once I was clean and dressed in some spare clothes that had been thoughtfully left at the terminal, I walked back into the main room where everyone was drinking coffee.

I grabbed a mug and perched on the arm of a chair while I waited for Lyall to bring us a car from the garage.

"How many cars do we have here?" I asked Artair.

"Just two," he replied.

I nodded. "Pen thought of everything, didn't she?"

Freya smiled. "She's a smart lady. That's why we need her back here, Flora."

I heard the car pull up outside, and I put my mug down before taking hold of the blood-stained blade. It had dried to a rusty red colour now, but I figured we could use warm water to soak it off.

"We'll be back soon, okay." I gave Enid and Freya a hug and nodded to the others.

"Be careful. We'll keep doing what research we can on the internet," Enid said.

If Castle Dion had burned, then so had all of our manuscripts. We had nothing on paper to help us now. I pushed the depressing thought to the back of my mind and headed out into the grey half-light of early morning.

I climbed into the car next to Lyall, and he started the drive to the hospital.

After a couple of minutes of silence, I asked the question that had been burning at the back of my mind.

"What happened after we left? Where's Leah?"

Lyall's jaw tightened, and his knuckles whitened as he gripped the steering wheel. For a moment, I thought he wouldn't answer me, but then he relaxed his grip and started to speak.

"I went back but everyone was out of the castle before I got there. I didn't see any of the others, except Leah. I found her in the gardens, but she tried to run from me. When I caught up with her, she admitted that she was the one who had left the gate open."

My eyes widened. I hadn't got to know Leah really well, but she had still been with us for months now. "How could she betray us?"

Lyall's lip pulled back in a snarl that reminded me of his wolf alter. "She was conditioned to being one of Sluag's minions, I guess. She'd spent too long around evil that she couldn't make the transition over from the dark side."

"What happened to her?" For a brief moment, dark thoughts invaded my mind.

He frowned at me. "I didn't hurt her, if that's what you thought. I let her go to the Draugur. It was what she wanted. I ran before they could get their claws into me, so I have no idea what happened after that."

I stared out of the window. The rain had finally stopped, but the sky was still overcast and grey. "What about Castle Dion? How badly did it burn?"

"The main structure is stone, love, so it will still be standing. The problem wasn't the fire, the problem was the fact the Supers seem to have decided to make it their home." His voice was husky, as though he was holding back his grief.

My lower lip quivered. "They're living there?"

He nodded but didn't speak.

I frowned. "What about the cats? Did you see Achilles?"

He nodded. "I saw all three of them, but they ran when I tried to get close. They know how to hunt, Flora, and they have each other. They'll be okay until we can get back to Castle Dion."

I was relieved Achilles and the other cats had escaped. But the thought of Supers living in the castle and possibly even sleeping in my room, devastated me. Especially when I thought of the state of the railway terminal I had just left the others hiding inside.

"What are we going to do?" My voice was barely a whisper.

He reached out and laid a reassuring hand on top of my own. "We're gonna make Pen well again, regroup, and then take our castle back. Don't worry, love, it's going to be okay."

I looked out the window as the hospital came into view, hoping with all of my heart Lyall was right.

Finlay met us at the door of the hospital and guided us to Pen. When I stepped into the room and saw her, my heart sank. She looked as though she had lost half her bodyweight overnight, she was hooked up to so many machines and drips, and she was unconscious.

I looked at Finlay. "I had no idea she was this sick."

He sat down next to Pen and wrapped one of her fragile hands in his own. "She's been unconscious all night. They haven't said it, but the hospital staff have given up on her."

I had texted Finlay to let him know we had the blood and that we were on the way. I just hadn't told him how exactly I got it. I drew the knife from my bag and unwrapped it from the protective plastic that it had been placed in.

"I just hope it's enough," I said.

Finlay's eyes widened as he took in the knife and the blood that tipped the end of the blade, but he didn't ask any questions, and I was grateful.

I located a kettle on a table in the corner of the room and flicked the switch to turn it on. Next, I stood the knife up in a cup and waited for the water to boil.

I poured the water along the blade, once the kettle had clicked itself off, and I was relieved to see the blood running into the glass along with the water. I tried not to pour too much water, knowing it was going to be a challenge to get Pen to drink even a small amount.

Once I was ready, I turned toward the bed, clutching the cup of swirling red liquid.

I prayed this was going to work.

CHAPTER 12

Finlay tenderly lifted Pen's head, and I poured the tiniest drop down her throat. I held my breath, hoping I hadn't misjudged and sent the liquid down her windpipe.

Pen's swallow reflex automatically kicked in, and she gulped the blood solution back. Encouraged, I poured a little more into her mouth, and she swallowed again.

"It's working. She's drinking it," Lyall murmured.

Once all of the liquid had disappeared down Pen's throat, Finlay laid her head back against the pillows, and we waited to see what would happen.

The first indication the blood had worked was a slight movement in the fingers of Pen's left hand. None of us spoke; we just waited to see if she would open her eyes.

When Pen's eyes flickered open, each of us smiled in relief. Finlay squeezed her hand gently, and I could see her fingers weakly return the gesture.

"Welcome back." Lyall said softly.

"What did you three do?" Pen's voice was quiet, but I could still hear her question in the silence of the room.

I gave her a brief rundown of everything that had happened since we evacuated Castle Dion, finishing with me using the kettle to create the blood solution and feed it to her.

Pen grimaced when she realised she had drunk Sluag's blood, and I eyed her apologetically.

"I'm sorry, it's not really as though we had a choice."

"I might not be in a position to tell you off too fiercely right now, Flora, but be assured I am furious with you for taking the risk you did to get Sluag's blood. However, I am grateful you did." She was looking better by the minute.

"Do you feel as though you're healed, Pen? We weren't sure there was enough." Finlay asked worriedly.

Pen shrugged. "I don't know. I feel better, but I think we will have to wait for the doctor to tell us if I'm completely free of the aneurysm."

"Perhaps we'll be able to get you out of here before too much longer." Lyall was enthusiastic.

Pen smiled morosely. "I'm in no rush to get to that railway terminal. I'm sorry it's not what you're used to, Flora."

"I don't mind it. I just want to take our castle back from the Supers," I said angrily.

"There is something I need you to do, before you do anything else," Pen admitted.

"Whatever you need, we'll do it." Finlay beamed at her.

Pen sat up a little straighter in the bed, and I was delighted to see a flush of colour in her cheeks.

"A week or so ago, I came across some information in one of the manuscripts I was studying. Apparently, there is a box stored in the Edinburgh library that can capture souls."

I blinked. "So, we can capture all of the rogues inside it?"

"Not quite," she admitted. "It can only house one soul at a time."

"No offence, Pen, but that doesn't sound massively useful to us." Lyall said what we were all thinking.

"If that one soul was Sluag's, then I think it could be extremely useful to us," Pen said hopefully.

My eyes were wide. "Do you honestly think that's possible, Pen? I mean, how do we even kick Sluag's soul out of his body?"

Pen gave a small shrug. "I hadn't got that far, which was why I hadn't mentioned my discovery to any of you yet."

"But you think it might be possible?" Lyall's voice held a tremor of excitement.

Pen nodded. "I do. I definitely think Flora will need you to share your energy with her, Lyall. But, the reason I'm telling you about this now is because the manuscript that gave me the information is still inside Castle Dion. If Sluag's Draugur are in control of the castle now, they might find the information and try to get hold of the box themselves."

"We need to get to it before they do," Finlay said determinedly.

"We do. Although, I'm afraid you won't be able to go along, Finlay." Pen didn't look my best friend in the eye when she spoke.

"Because of this body?" Finlay gestured at himself with a look of disgust.

Pen nodded sadly. "I'm afraid the storage facility for the manuscripts is spelled to prevent a Draugur from entering. I know you don't have the soul of a Draugur, but you do have the body of one, Finlay."

"It's not a big deal. I should stay here with you anyway, Pen." His face was flushed as he spoke, and my heart hurt for him.

"So, Flora and I need to leave as soon as possible." Lyall stood up.

"Not so fast, you should take two of the other Dion with you. If the Draugur are headed to the library, then you might run into them on the road." Pen held her hand up in a stop gesture as she spoke.

"Fair enough," Lyall conceded. "I'm not taking Freya and Bear, though. They are a nightmare together."

I snorted laughter. "The problem is that they aren't together. If they were, then I think they'd both be a lot happier."

"Tell that to Freya," Finlay grinned.

"Okay, Artair and Enid it is then. Freya and Bear can continue to hunt Draugur in the mortal world, and Finlay will stay with me," Pen said, settling the debate.

"How do we know we're going to be able to put Sluag in the box, though?" Lyall said, voicing what we all thought.

"We don't, but right now, this is the closet I've got to finding a way to stop him permanently," Pen admitted.

"All we can do is hope that it works, I guess." I watched a grimace of pain move across Pen's face, and I raised an eyebrow. That was not the face of someone who was totally cured.

Pen noticed my concern and smiled valiantly. "It's going to take a while for the symptoms to subside. Give it time, Flora."

I smiled, unconvinced. "Okay. We should let you get some rest, and we should probably do the same ourselves."

Lyall hooked his fingers through mine. "You must be exhausted. You haven't slept in a day."

"I'm not going to leave Pen's side. Hopefully we might get out of the hospital before too much longer." Finlay sounded positive.

My eyes met Pen's, and she held my gaze longer than I would have liked. We both knew it wasn't enough. I hadn't cured her, just given her a little longer. My mind ran frantic with thoughts of how I could get more of Sluag's blood.

"Neither of you are to take any unnecessary risks, do you understand me?"

I knew she had read my mind and was warning me not to go back to see Sluag again. In reality, her warning was pointless. I was certain he knew I hadn't taken enough blood, and I was certain he was expecting me to go back with my tail between my legs. The problem was, he wouldn't let me get so close next time—or if he did, he would be ready to crush me.

"I understand," I said quietly.

"You know I won't let anything happen to her, Pen." Lyall's

easy confidence made me thankful for him.

"In the meantime, Pen and I can try and work out ways to possibly support you with extra energy so that you can try and dislodge Sluag's soul without hurting yourself," Finlay said, sounding determined.

I smiled at him. "Thank you." I looked around the room at each of them before continuing. "But I want you all to know that I will do whatever it takes to end Sluag and stop him from getting into the world."

Lyall gripped my hand tightly as he spoke. "Except dying, love. You're not going to be doing any of that."

I held my head high and fixed my most determined look on my face, before replying. "If it comes down to me or him, then yes, Lyall, even dying is on the agenda."

"It's not going to come to that," Pen insisted before Lyall could reply.

I smiled warmly at her and my heart hurt. I wasn't ready to say goodbye to this amazing woman, who had spent so long in my life. I didn't think I would ever be ready to let her go.

"Let's hope it never comes to that," I agreed.

CHAPTER 13

We were both silent on the drive back to the terminal. I was lost amongst thoughts of losing Pen. My mind kept trying to think of ways to get hold of more of Sluag's blood, but every single idea ended up with me getting myself killed this time around. I'd had my window of opportunity, and I had completely screwed it up by not getting more.

Tears welled up in my eyes, and I rubbed them angrily.

"Flora, just so you know, I'm not quiet because I'm angry with you. What's wrong?" His voice was filled with concern.

If he didn't realise Pen was still sick, I wasn't going to be the one to make him face it just yet. "Nothing, I think I'm just really tired. It's been a hell of a night."

He nodded and seemed to be trying to decide whether or not to speak again. Eventually he seemed to come to a decision.

"I'm your Dion, Flora, and apart from that, we're bonded. I know I've only known you for less than a year and compared to how long you've been friends with Finlay, that's no time at all."

I started to interrupt him, wanting to tell him we didn't need to go through the whole Finlay argument again, but he growled at me and carried on talking.

"No, Flora. I need to tell you this because you need to know how important it is that you live."

I nodded silently and gave him my full attention.

"I know you want to go back and try to get more blood. I'm not an idiot, love. I know it wasn't enough and so does Finlay."

I raised my eyebrows in surprise. I had misjudged both of them.

Lyall gave me a wry smile. "We're not as stupid as we seem, sometimes. But, the problem is that there's no guarantee you'll come back next time, not now that Sluag knows what you want and what you're prepared to risk to get it."

He said the words that had been plaguing my mind since we had left the hospital. "I know," I whispered.

"We'll do everything we can to help Pen, love. I swear it. But, your safety isn't just important to us, it's paramount to the protection of the whole world. I can't let you take a risk like that again. If I had been here, you wouldn't have had the opportunity to try." He frowned as he concentrated on the road.

I wanted to fire back a smart-ass comment about how I was a modern-day woman, and I'd do what I needed to, but I bit it back. Lyall was right; this was so much bigger than my ego.

"I won't go back for his blood, Lyall. I swear." I said it honestly, knowing it was pointless to try anyway.

He nodded, seeming satisfied. Then he spoke again.

"I know it seems as though the only way to stop Sluag could mean you killing yourself, trying to force his soul of his body, but I can't let that happen, Flora."

"That's different," I argued. "Getting his soul in that box will save humanity from him, Lyall. If it comes down to giving up myself or the world, then I choose me, every single time."

His hands went white at the knuckles as he gripped the steering wheel, and I felt tears burn my eyes again.

"Not going to happen, love," he ground out through a clenched jaw.

I blinked through my tears.

"I don't want to die, Lyall. I only just found you, and it's crazy because I'd never even really thought about falling in love with someone before. I'd always just assumed that would happen in the future—you know at some point during one of those decades that I had left to experience in life."

I watched a single tear trace down his cheek as he determinedly kept his focus on the road ahead, and I fought back my own tears to continue.

"I know how much energy it takes to push a Super from its body, and Sluag's soul has been locked inside him for thousands of years. I don't even know if I'm going to be strong enough to do it. But, I do know that I have to try, and I have to give absolutely everything when I do, Lyall. If I can't get rid of him and the veil breaks, he'll destroy the world and everyone in it. I can't let that happen to anyone, including you."

"You know I'm going to give you every single, last drop of

energy I have to try and stop you from killing yourself, don't you?" His voice was hoarse.

I nodded. "I know. You can't force me to take it, though. I'll stop before it hurts you."

He punched the steering wheel, and I flinched at his anger.

"Flora, without you there's *no* life for me. My whole existence has consisted of a dead father, a mother who despised me, and a man I murdered before his kid could get to know him. If you die, I want to die too. There's nothing for me in this world without the brightness of your soul in it."

I bit my lip as he pulled the car up outside the front of the terminal, and we both climbed out. I was grateful to notice it still wasn't raining.

We stood facing each other, an unspoken agreement passed between us that the others didn't need to hear this, so we stayed where we were.

"I love you, Lyall. I never imagined anyone could make me feel the way that you do. It's as though I could take on a thousand Sluag's with you next to me." I reached out with my hand and wrapped his fingers in mine before continuing.

"That's why I have to do it. If Sluag breaks through the veil, he'll come for you before anyone else, because he knows what you mean to me. So, if I don't stop him, then I lose you anyway."

He frowned. "You've already accepted this haven't you?"

Trying to calm my aching heart, I stepped toward him, and he captured my face with his hands before leaning down to rest his forehead against mine.

"Yes," I whispered. "I've realised that no matter what happens, I was always going to have to say goodbye to you. It's just a question of which way it ends. But, I will trade my life to make sure that you don't lose yours."

His wolf eyes burned into mine. "I can't let that happen, love," he growled.

I leaned forward and pressed my lips against his before whispering. "I won't let you die. I love you too much."

He pulled back from me and narrowed his eyes at me. "Ditto," he said softly.

My green eyes stared unblinkingly into his amber wolf-eyes for what felt like an eternity. It was a stalemate, and we both knew it. He finally dropped his gaze from mine, and catching my hand, pulled me toward the terminal.

"We need to sleep if we're going to Edinburgh." His sudden subject change sent relief flooding through me.

He tugged me through the door of the terminal. It was quiet inside, and I realised the others must still be asleep. Lyall pushed open a door to a bedroom and stepped inside, still holding on to my hand.

I resisted a little. "I should probably find my own room."

He tilted his head. "So you can run off and try to get yourself killed again. No chance, Flora. From now on, you don't leave my sight."

I began to half-heartedly argue. The truth was, I didn't want to spend a second of the time we had left apart, anyway.

He cut me off. "Non-negotiable, love."

I nodded and allowed him to close the door on the rest of the world, determined that for a few hours, I would forget about everything except my wolf-eyed Dion, whose soul was and always would be mine.

CHAPTER
14

I woke up in a haze of confusion and darkness. I had no idea where I was or what time it was, before I suddenly realised Lyall had his arms wrapped around me, pulling my body against his chest, and I relaxed.

The reason it was so dark was because I was in the railway terminal, and the room had no windows. I picked up my phone and checked the screen to see what time it was, and I was surprised to see it was seven in the evening. My sleeping pattern was clearly wrecked.

I unwrapped myself from Lyall's arms and stood up to flick the switch on the dim light. The movement woke him, and he grinned up at me. "How did you sleep?"

"Better than I thought I would," I admitted.

He nodded. "We needed it, love."

I heard noises from the main room and nodded to the door. "We should catch up with the others and let them know what's going on."

"Lead the way, love." He crossed the room as he spoke, and we followed the smell of coffee until we were surrounded by the others.

Freya was lounging in a rickety wooden chair as we walked out of the bedroom, and she fired me a smirk before sipping from her cup. I rolled my eyes and ignored her, choosing to head toward the kitchen and pour myself a coffee. Lyall sat at the table and started talking with Artair.

"There's a few things we need to tell you all," I said as I sat down at the table.

"There's something we need to show you," Artair replied.

I frowned, not knowing if this was going to be good or bad. "Do you want to go first?" I asked.

Artair and Enid stood but Freya stayed seated. "I'll leave you guys to it. I'm going to grab a shower."

Artair and Enid led Lyall and me through the front door and around the back of the terminal building until we reached a large shed that must have housed trains way back when this line was still in use.

I looked at Lyall questioningly, but he just shrugged and followed the other two Dion. Artair reached the shed door and started to push it open.

"They just started showing up last night, while you were at the hospital," Enid said.

As the door pushed completely open, my eyes went wide with shock as I took in the figures of dozens of Draugur milling around the huge open space inside the shed.

"What the hell?" Lyall managed to find his voice.

"They all came to the terminal and swore their allegiance to Flora," Enid replied as she stepped into the shed.

The Draugur seemed to suddenly realise we were there, and every one dropped to their knees and bowed their heads. The one nearest to us spoke up on behalf of the others.

"We are here to sserve you, Ssoul Keeper."

I looked around the room in amazement. "My blood, it worked then?"

"It must have," agreed Artair.

"So, what do we do with them?" I asked as I approached the Draugur that had spoken. He was standing now, waiting patiently to hear what I would say.

Lyall was grinning. "They're your army, love. They might not be able to kill Sluag, but they can protect you when it comes down to getting his soul into that box."

"They can also kill Sluag's mortal world Draugur, just like we can," Enid supplied.

"Wait a minute. What box?" Artair gave us a confused look.

I felt a rush of positivity that had definitely been missing last night. Finally, something had happened in our favour.

"That's what we need to tell you. But we need everyone together. Let's go back to the terminal," Lyall answered.

"Will they be okay here?" I gestured at the Draugur as I spoke.

Artair nodded. "No matter what side they're on, they're still dead, Flora. They only need basic food or drink, and they don't care about whether or not we are nice to them. They just want to sserve you," he joked.

I punched his arm lightly and laughed. "Hey, don't upset my army."

"Wouldn't dream of it. Now tell us about this box?" Artair said curiously.

Freya collected Bear—who had still been in bed—and we all sat down at the long, spindly-legged table in the main room while Lyall and I recounted everything that had happened the night before.

The only thing we failed to tell the other Dion, was that Pen was still sick. Before we had gone to sleep, we had agreed to keep it between us for now. It seemed pointless to upset the others when we had so many things to focus on.

When we finished telling them everything, Bear leaned back in his chair and tried to casually drape his arm across the back of Freya's chair. She snorted at him, and he quickly pulled his arm back before speaking.

"So, when do we leave for Edinburgh?"

"You aren't leaving," Lyall replied.

"If you're going up against Draugur, don't you want a bear-shifter to help you out?" He waggled his eyebrows as he spoke.

Bear was a pretty terrifying shifter. He was huge when he changed into his animal alter—standing at almost ten feet tall on his hind legs. I knew that even wolf Lyall wouldn't stand a chance against his strength.

"You and Freya can do more damage by staying here and

hunting the mortal world Draugur. You could try taking the Flora-loyal Draugur with you. We're going to take Artair and Enid with us, which should be plenty of tooth and claw power." Lyall's voice was firm.

"I'm getting left here, with *him*?" Freya's voice was pitchy.

"Don't worry, hotness. I'll take care of you." Bear gave an exaggerated wink at Freya as he spoke.

"I actually hate you both," Freya hissed at Lyall and me.

I smiled affectionately at her and mouthed the word *sorry*.

"Are we leaving now?" Artair was all business.

"As soon as everyone is ready, yeah," I replied.

"Will we go in shifter form?" Enid asked.

"I think that would be best. We're more likely to go unnoticed that way, and we can eat on the move," Lyall agreed.

"Eww." Enid's face paled at the mention of wild food. "I'll shift into an eagle if that's all right with you guys?"

I smiled at her eagerness to fly by Artair's side as an eagle. "I think that's a good idea. You two can be our eyes up above. You have more chance of seeing any enemies approaching from the air."

Enid nodded in relief and headed to her room to clean up before we left.

"We shouldn't be gone more than five days. Can you guys check in on Pen and Finlay as well, please?" Lyall asked.

"Of course, we will." Bear spoke in a much more serious tone than he usually adopted.

Lyall nodded his thanks, and we both stood up. It was time

to go.

Freya and Bear walked outside with us to say goodbye.

"Be careful," Freya whispered to me as she hugged me tightly.

"I will, you too," I murmured.

Artair and Enid squealed with impatience from their perches on a lightning-struck tree. They had already changed, and were obviously ready to go.

"Pen's friend at the library is expecting us. As soon as we're back in human form, we'll use his phone to call you with an update, okay?" Lyall shifted from foot to foot as he spoke to Bear and Freya, clearly impatient to change form.

Freya nodded. "We'll be fine, Lyall. Now go and get that box so we can put Sluag down, permanently."

Lyall grinned at me. "I'll race ya?"

It took no longer than three seconds for us both to explode into a mass of black and white fur and begin galloping for the woods. I felt a hint of pride that I could finally match his shifting speed. Although I realised I'd never match his pace when he ran as a wolf as I saw his black tail disappear into the tangled woods before me.

Behind us, I could just make out the screeches of Artair and Enid as they dived from their perches and started to follow us in the air.

CHAPTER 15

If we weren't travelling under the fear of being discovered by Draugur, and I wasn't consumed with worry about Pen, I would have enjoyed our time together as our shifter selves.

I already knew I loved to run with Lyall in my wolf form, but I quickly discovered I loved being able to communicate with the two eagles who soared above our heads too, especially since they could pick out danger from miles away.

After two days of uninterrupted travel, we had become a bit complacent about the Draugur threat. As we approached Edinburgh, Lyall and I were in fierce competition—setting target finish lines and then racing each other to them. He would always win, unless I could manage to pick out an easier route through the terrain which meant I got less tangled in tree roots than him.

I had just beaten him to a river crossing that had been our latest finish line, and I was triumphantly pawing the soft ground of the riverbank when Enid's voice shot through my head.

Draugur. Closer than they should be. Dammit, we should

have been paying more attention.

Lyall reached my side and growled in frustration.

We should have been more alert. How far, how many, and in what direction, Enid?

The two eagles pitched and soared in the blue skies above us as they watched the approaching creatures that neither myself nor Lyall could see for ourselves.

South. They're only about half a mile away, and they're heading right for us. There's three of them in total.

I could sense Lyall debating what we should do, and I stayed quiet, giving him a moment to think.

He finally came to a decision.

Let's head east a little. We should be able to skirt around them as long as you two can keep eyes on them and make sure they don't change direction.

The eagles completed a full circle in the air above our heads before they glided in a southerly direction to keep track of the approaching Draugur.

Lyall lowered his head and bounded into the trees, heading east and away from the potential confrontation. After an uneasy glance over my shoulder, I bunched my muscles and leapt after him.

Lyall ran slowly enough to make sure I kept up with him, and we maintained an easy pace through the dim forest as we ran east, hoping we had acted quickly enough to avoid the oncoming Draugur.

None of us was particularly afraid of taking on three

Draugur, but every fight was a risk and could also draw unwanted attention to our current location.

Are they still headed in the same direction, Artair? Lyall's question sounded loud inside my head.

Yes, we're overhead and have all three Draugur in sight. Looks like you've missed them completely. We'll watch them for another mile and then catch up with you guys. We might lose range on communication for a bit, though.

Lyall shrugged his huge black shoulders at Artair's reply.

No big deal, you'll find us again in no time. See you soon.

There was no reply from either Artair or Enid, and I guessed they had moved out of range of our telepathic link. I shook off a shiver of worry and followed Lyall's lead.

He had started to curve our direction around a little. Now that we were out of the path of the Draugur, we were gradually realigning ourselves southward bound.

I hope they're okay.

They're fine. They have wings, love. The Draugur can't touch them.

I nodded my head, knowing he was right. We were the only ones who would have been in danger if the Draugur spotted us.

We ran in mental silence for another few minutes before Lyall suggested we stop and wait for the eagles to catch up with us. We halted by a stream and both took advantage of lapping at the cool, fresh water while we waited.

I had just lifted my head after finally satisfying the thirst that burned at the back of my throat, when a blur of colour flew through the air and knocked into Lyall, taking him by surprise and toppling him off his huge paws.

I had no time to react before a second Draugur barrelled into my side, catching me unawares. We both snarled and snapped at our attackers. Even now, I wasn't particularly worried about taking on two Draugur. With Lyall at my side, they had no chance.

When six more of the creatures suddenly burst from the tree line, my heart almost dropped in my chest, and fear rose like bile at the back of my throat.

Lyall. There's more of them. I shouted inside my mind.

Artair? Enid? Lyall howled inside my head.

There was nothing, no answer from either of the other Dion. There was nothing we could do except keep on fighting and hope we could hold the Draugur off until the others eventually arrived.

Lyall sank massive teeth into the leg of the first Draugur that had attacked him and was rewarded with a yelp of pain. He turned excitedly in my direction.

Flora, they're mortal world Draugur. We can kill them.

I sent up a silent thank you that our opponents weren't Endwood Draugur, as without the power of speech, I couldn't have sent them back to where they belonged. These guys, however, could be torn apart by wolf jaws, and they wouldn't ever make a comeback.

With renewed energy, I lunged toward my attacker and locked my jaws around her throat before tearing my head back.

I had such strength as a wolf, that I almost split her head from her body.

For a sickening second, my mind was overwhelmed by the image of Helena Harris, with her throat torn open in the same way, and I froze.

I had finally learned to accept I had no choice in killing Lyall's mother. But, I was still haunted by images of what I had done. Every now and again, the scene would play out in my mind and torment me with guilt. Now, really wasn't the time to let it take over my mind, however.

My hesitation cost me dearly, and I felt a searing pain as a second Draugur plunged a silver blade into my shoulder.

Flora? Lyall howled in rage as he tried to fight his way past three more of the Draugur who crawled over him like ants.

I quickly glanced down to see a bloom of red saturating my snow-white coat as the Draugur pulled its blade free and allowed the wound to bleed. The pain served as motivation, and I leapt at the Draugur, taking it to the ground with a thud and tearing at its flesh.

Another Draugur wrapped its arms around my neck from behind me and started to squeeze in an attempt to cut off my air supply. I wriggled and bucked, trying to throw it off my back, and I was suddenly afraid they might actually kill us both.

A sudden shriek announced the arrival of Artair and Enid. As Artair dived at the eyes of the Draugur that was strangling me, Enid pecked at the face of one of Lyall's attackers.

Artair quickly won his battle with the Draugur on my back,

and I huffed in ragged breaths of air as it released its grip on my throat and fell away from me to land on the ground.

Flora, you're bleeding. Artair's voice inside my head was thick with worry.

Lyall reached my side and effortlessly finished off the last two standing Draugur with Enid's help. His fury was so strong that nothing could have stood against him, but when he reached my side, his whole demeanour changed, and he whimpered softly as he licked at the wound on my shoulder.

I'm okay. I don't think it's too deep. I tried to reassure them all.

Enid was perched on a broken log, her yellow-gold eyes focussed on the forest edges as though she expected more Draugur to attack.

We need to get moving. It's only about four miles to the library, and I think Flora needs to get that wound treated.

Lyall stood before me and bowed his head remorsefully.

I'm so sorry, love. I should have realised there could be more of them. I shouldn't have let both of the others leave. Now you're hurt.

I started limping south. I was surprised at how painful my shoulder was now, and I was more than a little bit worried about the amount of blood I had lost.

It's okay, Lyall. None of us knew. Come on, we need to get to the library.

The eagles took to the sky, hovering directly above us—not letting us out of their sight again. Lyall stayed so close to my side

98

as we walked I could feel the rumbling vibrations of every breath he took.

CHAPTER 16

As the library loomed into view, I took a moment to be thankful the gothic structure had been built on a stretch of greenery on the outskirts of Edinburgh and not in the centre of the city.

Even with the protection of the twisting and winding little alleyways that made up the network of tiny streets in the old town, I knew I was in too much pain to be stealthy enough to avoid the gaze of hundreds of city dwellers. Add that to my bright, white fur, and I wouldn't have stood a chance of going unnoticed.

The library rose up from the immaculately sculpted gardens which sprawled around the gothic structure. Its individual spires pointed toward the sky like elaborately decorated fingers, and the cast-iron drainpipes fed rainwater to the waiting mouths of hideously graphic gargoyles, who leered down at us from their eternal perches on the building corners.

It's an impressive building, Lyall admitted as we

approached the huge double doors.

It's creepy, Enid thought aloud as she hesitantly landed on a stone dragon that was one of a pair that appeared to guard the entrance.

The doors swung open, and just as I was wondering how we were going to communicate with the round and red-faced man who appeared from behind them, he spoke.

"Welcome, Soul Keeper and her Dion. There will be time for formalities later. You are hurt, Flora Bast. Come inside and let's get that wound fixed up."

The two birds of prey flew through the door and into the huge open library space, and Lyall and I followed quickly after them, crossing the black and white checked floor.

Once I was inside and I knew we were safe, I permitted myself to fall to the floor. My tongue lolled from my mouth as I panted heavily.

Flora? Lyall's fear was obvious, even inside my head, but I had no energy to reply. Instead, I burrowed my nose into my fur and let blissful unconsciousness wash over me.

Waking up in a camp bed inside a tiny wood-panelled room that was furnished with a single desk and about a thousand books, I sat up quickly as I realised I was back in human shape and wearing clothes.

Lyall's voice felt like a soothing balm across my bandaged shoulder.

"Hush, love, you're all right."

"Lyall, how did I get here? Who dressed me?" The only

thing I cared about right now was who had seen me without my clothes.

He snickered a little. "Stop panicking, Flora. Enid dressed you. Your dignity is still intact."

I breathed out a sigh of genuine relief and lay back against the lumpy pillow. "What happened?"

He leaned across the bed and grabbed my hand, twining his fingers with mine. He lifted my hand gently and teased his lips against my knuckles before he replied.

"You'd had too much, love. You passed out, and when that happens, you shift back to human form. Eric dressed the wound. He's a bit of a witch doctor, I think, and then he put you in his room to rest."

I looked around the book-crammed room sceptically. "This is where he sleeps?"

"He *is* a librarian, Flora," Lyall laughed. "So, how do you feel?"

I shifted my shoulder and realised the pain was almost completely gone. "I feel good. I wouldn't mind a shower, though."

"I thought you might say that. I'll show you were to go, and then you can meet us down in the library stacks, love."

I swung my legs out of the bed and stood up to follow Lyall. As we padded along the threadbare carpet of the balcony that followed all four walls of the building and overlooked the library down below, something occurred to me.

"Did you get the box?"

Lyall pushed open the door to the tiny but immaculately kept shower room. "No, Eric said he will only give it to you. Apparently, he needs to give you instructions to go with it."

I shrugged. "That makes sense, I guess."

"See you downstairs, love." He headed for one of the three staircases that wound their way down to the library floor.

"Okay, see you in a minute." I closed the door behind me and hurriedly showered and brushed my teeth with a toothbrush I found that was labelled *Flora*.

Once I was dressed, I padded down the same staircase Lyall had used and crossed the buffed and polished stone of the floor to reach the huge, round table where the others were waiting.

The red-faced man who had opened the front door to us was seated at the table, and he smiled as I sat. I guessed this was Eric, and I returned his smile.

"Thank you for fixing my shoulder up, Eric."

He ducked his head in acknowledgement. "It was nothing, Flora. We are here to help you in any way we can at the Library of the Anam. We may not be fighters, but we are known to be healers and avid students."

"Did Pen tell you everything when she called?" I wondered if he knew just how close to the end of the world we were.

He nodded sagely. "She did, although we already knew much of it anyway."

"Really? How so?" Lyall asked curiously.

Eric raised his white eyebrows, making his jowly face look even more friendly. "We are an establishment of knowledge,

Lyall. We employ a lot of seers."

It was our turn to raise our eyebrows at that. "So, you have knowledge of the future then?" Artair quizzed.

"Some," Eric replied evasively.

"Do you know anything that might help us fight Sluag?" Enid asked.

"Yes and no, young one. Seeing is subject to constant changes and influences. It isn't often we can guarantee our visions."

I was certain he was hiding something intentionally. "Do you have any information you can share with us?"

He paused and studied me for a long while before he finally answered me. "No."

"Oh." My disappointment was obvious.

"I do have information I can share with you, Flora, but only you."

"All right, when?" I asked, eager to hear what he had to say.

"I have some things I must attend to this afternoon. Once I am finished, we can talk. I'll send someone for you." He stood up to leave.

"What should we do in the meantime?" Enid asked.

Eric beamed at her and waved his arm at the stacks of books that surrounded us. "Every remaining Dion manuscript in existence is stored here. Read and learn."

After Eric left, Artair's mouth twitched in humour. "He's a little eccentric, isn't he?"

"I think he's lovely," Enid said kindly.

"I think he's hiding a ton of stuff from us," Lyall growled, his amber eyes burning as he stared in the direction Eric had taken.

"I agree," I murmured. "I'll find out what later, though."

Lyall tapped his fingers thoughtfully against the polished wood of the tabletop. "Make sure you push him, love. I want to know everything that could help us win this war."

Artair's voice pulled my attention away from Lyall's dark gaze. "So, where do we start with these manuscripts?"

I shrugged. "Truthfully, I don't think there's going to be enough time to find out very much. Once I get the information and the box from Eric, we need to get back to the terminal, so we can start planning how to get Sluag inside the box."

Lyall finally brought his attention back to our table. "Flora's right. As soon as she gets the box and the information, we're out of here."

"Talking of the terminal, I need to call the others and check on Pen." Enid stood up to go and make the call.

"I hope everyone back home is okay," I whispered as I watched Enid leave.

Lyall and Artair were both reaching for some of the manuscripts that were strewn across the centre of the table.

"Of course, they'll be okay, love. Bear won't let a thing happen to Freya, and Finlay has Pen's back." Lyall spoke with confidence.

I tapped my index finger distractedly against the dark green cover of a huge book. "I hope you're right," I said softly.

CHAPTER 17

We spent several hours in the atrium of the library, scouring every manuscript we could get our hands on. Enid returned from calling home to bring us the news that Freya and Bear were doing well and had a lot of success in using the converted Draugur to fight on their side.

The news from the hospital was more troubling. Pen was slipping away again. It seemed Sluag's blood was wearing off quicker than we had hoped. Lyall and I explained to the others that Pen probably didn't have much longer left, and it left a quiet cloud of sadness over our table.

So, I was half relieved and half nervous when a young librarian came to tell me Eric was ready to see me.

I followed the boy—who could only have been around fourteen—through the stacks until we reached a wooden door with a frame so low I had to duck to enter the stone room inside.

The boy closed the door behind me, and Eric gestured for me to sit down in a black wooden chair that, along with the table, took up almost all of the space in the tiny room.

There was a box sitting on the table-top that was around the size of a ring-box. It was carved of blue wood and engraved with hundreds of tiny flowers which I immediately recognised.

I reached out to touch the box in surprise and awe. "Those are the flowers from the Everwood."

Eric gently pushed the little box across the table toward me. "Well spotted, Flora. The box is made from the wood of a tree from the Everwood."

I frowned as I picked up the small box and studied it. "But, the trunks of the trees in the Everwood aren't blue. Just the flowers."

He smiled at me. "They are Síorraidh trees. On the outside, the bark looks like any ordinary tree. On the inside they are as blue as their flowers."

"Being from the Everwood gives the box the power to capture Sluag's soul," I mused.

Eric's voice was stern. "No, not the power to capture his soul, just to hold it for eternity. The power to capture it comes entirely from you, Flora."

I sensed he wanted to say more, and I suspected I wasn't going to like it when he did. But he changed the subject instead.

"Penthesilea is critically ill."

It wasn't a question but I answered him anyway. "Yes."

He nodded at me, his soft brown eyes filled with sadness. "We have seen the end for her, and it is not far away, Flora. You must prepare yourself."

I had known we were going to lose Pen, but some stubborn part of me had refused to believe it, until now.

"Can't we do something?" I whispered.

Eric spoke softly and with complete sincerity. "Child, what would you have us do? We are not here to change the natural order of things. In fact, you are here to do the exact opposite."

"I know but I need her, Eric." I bit my lip in an attempt to hold back the tears that threatened to fall.

He reached his hand out to cover my own, comfortingly. "You will have everyone you need with you, when the time comes."

Each time I grew a little more in confidence as a Soul Keeper, something happened to knock me right back down to the frightened little girl I became when I lost my parents.

Pen had stepped up and taken care of me when I had no one left in the whole world. She had done that for each and every one of us, and now I was supposed to just let her die.

I stared at the box that was gripped tightly in my hand and directed my rage in the only way I knew how. "How do I make sure I put Sluag in here?"

"I believe you already know that process, Flora. I wanted to speak with you alone because I needed to make sure you were fully aware of the cost." Eric squeezed my hand as he spoke.

His words made my blood run cold. "What will be the cost?" I asked quietly.

He withdrew his hand and sat up straighter in his chair. "I have consulted with all of our seers over and over again. They seem extremely confident that you will succeed in dislodging Sluag's soul and trapping him in the Síorraidh box."

I smiled weakly. "Well that's about the best news I've had all year, Eric."

He held up a hand. "That was the process, Flora. We are yet to discuss the cost."

My shoulders sagged, the injured one throbbing slightly. "Tell me?" I asked.

He looked at me thoughtfully for a moment before he spoke. "Remember there are no guarantees. What our seers have been shown may change with circumstance and because of the decisions you make."

"Eric?" I was fidgeting now.

"All right, Flora, but steel yourself. It seems that you truly are the Soul Keeper chosen by fate to end Sluag. But, the sacrifice for stopping Sluag's reign in the Endwood will cost most of you your lives."

I drew in a sharp breath. "How many is most?"

"I don't know, Flora. I honestly don't know."

I took several deep breaths before I asked my next question. "Do you know who?"

He was quiet for so long I was beginning to think he had forgotten how to speak. His eyes flickered as though there was a war of indecision going on behind them, and I knew he was trying to choose whether or not he told me the next part.

Finally, he spoke. "Lyall is almost certainly going to die, Flora."

All of the breath rushed out of me, my head started to spin, and I felt the cold trickle of nausea running up my throat which indicated my body's desire to pass out. I wanted to scream and cry and break things.

"No. There must be another way," I managed through my breathless throat. "If it comes down to me or him, then it can be me. I'm ready for that, Eric."

Eric looked at me pityingly. "It doesn't come down to you and him, Flora."

I narrowed my eyes. "What do you mean?" I growled.

"You already know how to stop the casualties of the coming war, Flora," Eric insisted.

I cast about frantically inside my mind, but I had no idea what he meant. All I could think was that I had to do whatever it took to stop Lyall from dying.

"I don't know what you're talking about, Eric. Tell me what to do?"

"If you stop the veil from being torn down, then Sluag won't come to the mortal world, and you will have no need to fight him at a disadvantage." Eric spoke so quietly I had to lean forward to hear him.

Realisation dawned on me, and my world came crashing down around me. It was always going to come down to this, the choice between the life of my best friend and the life of the man I loved.

"Finlay," I whispered brokenly.

"I'm so sorry to do this to you, Flora, but if the Super

Draugur are destroyed then the veil will not fall and Lyall will almost certainly live."

"I can't choose between them, Eric. Don't make me do that," I whimpered.

Eric took both of my hands in his own and stared sadly at me. "You must choose. That is your responsibility and yours alone, Flora Bast. If you end Finlay's existence, then all of the other deaths will probably be avoided. If you let Finlay live, then you could lose many of your Dion, and you almost certainly *will* lose Lyall."

CHAPTER 18

I had returned to the library in a daze, clutching hold of the box as though my life depended on it. Enid and Artair were delighted we had everything we came for, but Lyall eyed me with suspicion from the minute I got back—he knew something was wrong.

I did the only thing I could think of. I closed myself off to everyone, including Lyall. I couldn't tell any of them what Eric had told me, because that would force me to face up to the decision I had to make.

Deep inside I was aware that I had probably made my decision before I left that tiny stone room, and I was sure that no one else would agree with me, which was why I kept my mouth shut.

As I had stood to leave, Eric had caught hold of my hand and pulled me close to him. He spoke with a quiet desperation.

"Flora, Finlay's host is failing. Even a Super Draugur body cannot contain a Dion's soul. There is no real choice to make.

After Finlay loses this body, there will be nowhere left for him to go. He will ask you to send his soul on anyway. All you are doing is speeding the process up."

I had torn my hand back from Eric's, fury filling every fibre of my body. "It's not the same thing, and you know it. You're asking me go back to the terminal and obliterate my best friend's soul like a rogue? I can't do that, Eric. I won't," I shouted.

He spoke calmly, despite my hysteria. "Flora, you have a future with Lyall. He is your bonded Dion. Everything is simply happening in the way it was fated to be. If you spoke to Finlay, I am certain he would offer his soul to stop Sluag from breaching the veil."

"You don't know what you're asking," I spat. "You said it yourself. All of the visions are subject to changes and the decisions we make. There are no guarantees either way that we will win. If there's even a small chance I can save both of them, then I have to try."

Eric shook his head sadly as I opened the door to the library. "If you don't act now, you may lose them both, Flora."

"Yeah? Well maybe I'm in the mood to take a gamble." I threw my parting words to Eric as I slammed the door behind me and left him still sitting at the small table.

The manuscripts hadn't told us anything we didn't already know, and so we decided to cut our losses and start the long journey home straight away.

Changing into my wolf shape was excruciatingly painful due to the wound on my shoulder. I had almost given up after five full minutes of trying to move through the phases and continually ending up on my knees in agony each time.

When I finally managed to shift, I was surprised and pleased to find that my wound didn't hurt so much. Once I had checked the collar that held the Síorraidh box was secured around my furry throat, I was grateful for the solitude inside my own head as we ran for the north.

Lyall ran next to me, and he kept shifting his gaze toward me and studying my face. I was grateful that wolf faces didn't betray emotions in anything like the same way a human face did.

Once or twice he tried to question me.

What happened with Eric, Flora?

I rolled my white shoulders in a shrug. *Nothing. We just didn't agree on the best course of action.*

Lyall huffed at that and continued pushing me. *He might have been giving you sound advice, love. He has an army of seers at his beck and call, after all.*

I growled, deep and low in the back of my throat. *He said it himself, it's all subject to change. None of it is guaranteed.*

Talk to me, Flora. Tell me what's upset you so much, please? He whined softly.

Lyall, I'm not doing this right now. Give me a little space, okay? I accelerated my pace and put a few metres between us. I chose to run this way for the rest of the journey, and although I could sense how hurt he was, Lyall didn't push me again.

After two days of pushing ourselves to the limits, we made it back to the terminal, and I was shocked by how relieved I was to see the dull and derelict frontage of the building we now called home.

Freya came out front to meet us, and I trotted over to her and lifted my head to give her access to the Síorraidh box beneath my chin. She unfastened the collar and turned the box over in her hands.

"Pretty."

I bobbed my head in a nod and bounded inside the terminal to get cleaned up. Lyall, Artair and Enid followed suit and before long, all six of us sat together around the battered and broken table.

"So, what did the librarians have to say?" Bear was sitting closer to Freya than I had ever seen him get, and I cocked an eyebrow inquisitively at the pair—something had changed while we were away.

Lyall answered him. "The box that Flora brought back will trap Sluag, and they seem to think that we have a good chance of stopping the end of the world."

Freya turned the box over and over in her hands. "So, the veil won't fall?"

I stayed silent, awash with guilt and shame.

"Afraid it's not that simple, Freya," Artair answered her. "It sounds as though the veil has to fall before we face Sluag for the final time."

"At least that's what the seers have been shown," Enid explained.

"Doesn't that mean that a lot of people could get hurt or

even die?" Bear asked.

"We're doing the best we can. What else do you want? More blood?" I snapped.

Freya frowned. "Whoa, there was no need for that, Flora. We're all worried about what's coming next, you know."

I bit my lip as Lyall gave me a concerned look. "Is everything okay, love. Why don't you tell us what Eric said to you?"

I narrowed my eyes at him. He was trying to put me on the spot in front of the others. He wanted to leave me no choice but to tell them all what Eric had told me.

I stood up so quickly my chair toppled backward and landed against the floor with a crash.

"There will be time for planning how to get Sluag into the box later. Have either of you been to visit Pen while we were away? Or were you too busy with each other?" I hated myself for how unfair I was being.

A look of anger flashed across Freya's face as she jolted her body farther away from Bear's.

"Yes, we've been to see her. She's dying, Flora, and there's nothing we can do about it."

Although it was only what I already knew, the words were like a slap across the face and a knife to my heart. *It's too soon. I'm not ready.*

A little of the anger left me, and my exhausted body sagged. "I'm sorry, Freya, all of you. I'm tired and my shoulder hurts like hell. I'm going to try and get a few hours of rest, and then I want to visit Pen."

Lyall stood. "I'll come with you."

I held my hand out toward him and shook my head. "I really need to take a bit of time to myself tonight, Lyall, okay?"

He was hurt, but he simply nodded and sat back at the table with the others as I crossed the room and clicked the bedroom door closed behind me.

I lay in the darkness for half an hour. I could hear the hum of voices from the other room. I knew the others were probably talking about me, but I couldn't make out any of what they were saying, and I probably didn't actually want to know.

Eventually I made my decision. Lyall had made me promise not to go back to the Endwood in person, but he hadn't said anything about going back in dream form. I closed my eyes and willed myself back to the grim landscape of Sluag's realm.

CHAPTER
19

Immediately, as I materialised in the Endwood, I realised something was different. The trees were still blackened and charred, and the grass remained the colour of ink. But the nighttime sky and the cold, yellow moon had been replaced with a crimson-coloured canopy that promised a coming dawn.

The fire of a new day blazed above me. Spears of rose-gold pierced through the blood-red clouds. It looked like how I would have imagined the skies of hell to look. If hell had existed.

"I didn't think I'd see you show your face here again, Flora."

I spun around to find Sluag sitting comfortably on a golden throne that absorbed the light of the sky above, as it nestled among the black grass.

"You've upgraded from your tree stumps." I gestured to the throne as I spoke.

He snickered. "Tree stumps are all well and good for The Host of the Unforgiven Dead. A throne is more satisfactory for the Ruler of Earth."

"You're not there yet, Sluag," I ground out through clenched teeth.

The grey-scaled monster raised his arms above his head in an all-encompassing gesture. "Look around you, Little Dreamer. It won't be long until I am the Lord of Everything."

I looked up at the sky and then dropped my gaze back to meet Sluag's eyes. "Why has the sky changed colour?"

He beamed at me in delight. "Won't you sit, Flora?" He gestured at the floor in front of him as he spoke.

"I'm good, thanks." I refused.

He shrugged. "Suit yourself."

I didn't reply. Instead, I waited patiently to hear him tell me what had changed within the Endwood.

Sluag sighed heavily. "Oh, Little Dreamer. You are less and less chatty by the day." He settled his elbow on the arm of the throne and brought his chin down to rest on his curled fist.

"I suppose tragedy does somewhat dull a human's ability to stay positive," he murmured thoughtfully.

"I'm not really human, though, am I?" I offered.

He considered me for a moment. Then, "Close enough."

I rolled my eyes. "The sky, Sluag?"

"It's simple really, Flora. The time of eternal night in the Endwood is over. It is a new dawn where rogue souls will be reborn into a world of my creation instead of coming here to die."

I barked laughter. "Or it's a new dawn because I'm going to destroy you, and everything about the Endwood will change for the better."

He raised a sparse brow and grinned. "You mean after you put me in to your little box?"

I shouldn't have been surprised that he knew about the Síorraidh box.

"You're right to be worried about it," I countered.

"Ha. You mistake me, Flora. I am not worried. I am entertained by your predicament."

So, he knew about the visions Eric had told me of.

"Of course, I know. I have my own little seer, remember, Flora?"

I scowled at his mention of Leah. "How is the traitor doing?"

"Serving her purpose until I no longer need her alive." He spoke so casually of killing Leah, it made me feel sick.

Suddenly, he stopped grinning and gripped the arms of his throne tightly with the long and bony fingers of both hands. Leaning forward, he focussed his oil-slick eyes on me.

"Tell me, why don't you put an end to your traitor in order to save the life of the one you claim to love, Little Dreamer?"

I snarled. "That's not up for discussion, Sluag."

He smiled, enjoying the burn from the nerve he'd hit. "Have you told Lyall that you're sacrificing him so that Finlay can have a few more pathetic days in the mortal world?"

"I've seen no proof that Finlay's body is failing this time, Sluag, and I have no intention of letting Lyall die. I *can* protect them both."

He tapped a finger thoughtfully against his chin as he watched me shift uncomfortably from foot to foot.

"If you're so certain of that, then why haven't you told your loyal followers the truth?"

And there it was. The question that had been tormenting my mind since Eric first told me about our future.

"I don't know," I admitted. I hated how easy it was to be honest with Sluag, although I suspected it had something to do with being in his world and not my own.

"You admit the truth to me because we are two halves of one whole, you and I, Flora. We need each other, just as light needs dark and dawn needs dusk. Love it or loathe it, we have a bond that overreaches even the one you have with Lyall, Little Dreamer."

I scrunched my face up in disgust. "We really don't."

"You'll see. If you somehow do manage to get me in that box, I believe you will mourn at the void I leave," he said confidently.

I huffed but didn't say anything.

"Anyway, truth be told, Flora, you can't get rid of Finlay's soul just yet," he said in an exaggerated stage-whisper.

"Why not?" He had my attention again now.

He shrugged. "Oh, just a little rumour I heard. But be assured that you might do a lot of damage to your campaign to save the world if you do get rid of him."

I needed to move past this chit-chat and get to the part where I begged him for his blood—for all the good it would do me.

"How so?" My voice was clipped and business like.

Sluag pouted. "It's no fun when you hide your emotions, Flora. But, I digress. Finlay is pivotal to your success in overthrowing my tyrannical plot to rule the world. Or at least, so I hear."

"Even if that was true, why would you tell me something that could help me defeat you?" I stood my ground.

"What did I just tell you, Flora?" Sluag rolled his eyes in apparent frustration. "We are part of the same purpose. You struggle to conceal the truth from me, as I fight to still my treacherous tongue around you."

What he told me made perfect sense. Sluag and I had always told each other the truth, despite the fact that we were always going to be on opposing sides.

If he was telling me the truth, then it was almost certain Lyall would die, and I would lose Finlay anyway.

"I am sorry to be the bearer of such bad tidings, Little Dreamer, but both of the men you love are going to die, and there isn't a thing you can do to stop it." Sluag sat back comfortably against his throne.

I couldn't think about this right now. If I did, I would crumble, and I had a reason to stay strong for just a little while longer.

I straightened my back and stared him down. "What would it take to make you give me your blood?"

Without hesitation, Sluag stood from the throne and in

three great strides was standing in front of me. He reached his bony fingers up to grab my chin, tightening his grip when I tried to yank my head back.

Leaning into my face he hissed each word slowly. "Give. Me. Lyall."

"No," I snarled.

Then, just like that, he released my chin, letting me stumble backward, as the tug of my resistance was no longer balanced by his grip.

"Then no deal, Flora Bast. No deal," he roared to the sky.

It was in moment that I finally allowed myself to feel the gut-wrenching acceptance that Pen would die, and I wouldn't be able to do a thing to stop it. All I could do now was wake myself up and go to say goodbye.

"I suspect this is the last time that you and I shall meet in this way, Little Dreamer," Sluag said sombrely as he resumed his seat on his throne.

"The next time we meet I *will* put you in that box, Sluag. And once you're in there, you are never, ever coming back out," I swore.

Sluag tapped his wrist as though pointing out an imaginary watch. "Tick, tock, Little Dreamer. She'll be dead before you get there at this rate."

Fury ripped through me as I began to fade from the landscape, and in the last instant that I saw his face—smiling in delight—I vowed to myself that no matter what else happened I would give everything, including my own life, to see him caged for eternity.

CHAPTER 20

I sat up in bed, gasping with rage. My fingers tore blindly at the bedsheets around me.

"Easy, love. You're all right." Lyall reached though the dim light of the room to lay a comforting hand against my cheek.

Without thinking, I threw myself forward and into his arms. I wrapped my own arms around his neck and buried my face in the dip between his collarbone and his neck, inhaling his familiar scent.

"I'm so sorry. I shouldn't have lashed out at you all."

He looked surprised by my sudden clinginess but held me tightly nonetheless. "What happened with Eric, Flora? Tell me?" he asked softly.

I pulled back from him and laid a gentle kiss against his cheek, before I started to climb out of bed. "I can't, not until I speak to Pen." I didn't add that this was probably the last chance I would get to draw on the older woman's wisdom.

"Do you want me to come with you?"

"No, I'll be in the car the whole way. I'll be fine." Something told me I needed to hurry, and so I pulled on my tan boots, and with a quick glance back at Lyall, I left the room to get the car.

Arriving at the hospital, I found Finlay asleep on a row of uninviting-looking chairs outside Pen's room. I looked around until I found a storage room and ducked inside to poach a blanket.

I returned to my best friend's forty-year-old body and laid the blanket over him gently. He murmured in his sleep but didn't wake. I breathed out a sigh of relief and pushed open the door to Pen's room.

Pen's eyes were closed when I walked into the dimly lit room, but they flickered open as soon as she heard my entrance.

"I thought you might be sleeping," I whispered as I sat next to the bed.

She smiled weakly. "No, I was waiting for you, Flora."

I closed my eyes in an attempt to hold back the tears that threatened to fall as I gently lifted Pen's hand and pressed it to my cheek.

"What am I going to do without you, Pen?"

She squeezed my hand. "You're going to put Sluag in that box and prevent the end of the world, I hope."

Laying Pen's hand back down against the crisp, white hospital sheets, I sat up a little straighter.

"Pen, Eric told me some stuff, and I'm scared I'm going to get it wrong."

Pen gave her head the slightest nod. "He told you to choose

between losing Finlay or Lyall."

I gave her a crestfallen look. "He called you and told you?"

"He did and I have to say I was upset with the way he told you, Flora. It's not fair to ask you to decide between the boy who has loved you for your whole life long and the man who is your future." Pen's voice was sympathetic.

"Sluag told me I can't stop him without Finlay. If that's true then Lyall will die. Does it really come down to sacrificing Lyall for the rest of the world? Because if it does, then I don't know if I'm the right person for the job, Pen," I confessed.

Pen placed her hand gently over mine. "I've seen the manuscript, Flora. Somehow and in some way, Finlay will play a part in bringing Sluag down."

"Then Lyall will die?" My voice came out sounding small and childlike.

"Perhaps not. Eric was right, these predictions are subject to change. One single decision that you make could change the course of events entirely."

"Perhaps isn't enough, Pen," I growled.

"Is perhaps enough to unleash hell on every single soul in the world? On all of those whom you are sworn to protect, Flora?" She didn't say it in an accusing way, but it still felt like a knife to my own soul.

"I can't let Lyall die." I turned wide eyes on her.

"You must talk to both Finlay and Lyall, Flora. Perhaps they should be given a chance to make their own decisions. We know you need Finlay to be there at the end, but perhaps we can keep

Lyall away from the final battle with Sluag."

I shook my head sadly. "I know him, Pen. He won't leave me to fight Sluag alone, and I'm pretty sure I can't dislodge Sluag's soul without Lyall's help, at least to start with anyway."

"They still deserve to know the truth." She reached out and grazed the back of her frail hand down my cheek, gently. "You've done so well since you found out who you were, Flora. Aiden was a truly outstanding Soul Keeper, but I think you will be a legendary one."

Tears pooled in my eyes. "I want to make the right choices, Pen, I really do."

"And you will, sweetheart but you must talk to your Dion. Otherwise they cannot help you." Pen's face twisted in pain, and I reached for the help button at the side of the bed.

"No, Flora." She stopped my hand in mid-air with her own.

"They can help you," I argued.

"They can drug me, but I need to keep my wits about me for a little longer. I must ask a favour of you, Flora." She spoke seriously.

"Anything."

"My time is short and when it comes, I don't want to live like Finlay—pushed from body to body. I'm asking you to let me go, Flora." Pen hissed in a sharp breath as she finished speaking.

"But, the Super Draugur body is working for Finlay. We could choose a body for you and you could stay. I need your guidance, Pen." The fear was evident in my voice.

Pen shook her head firmly. "Finlay would have you believe

that his body is okay. But, I've been with him these last few weeks, Flora. It's breaking apart, slower than the Draugur body but breaking apart nonetheless."

"Then Eric was telling the truth. There's nowhere else for Finlay to go?" My mouth was dry.

"No, sweetheart, there isn't, and that's why I can't let you do the same thing to me. I don't want that, Flora. I just want to be sent on to my new life like any other pure soul." She looked me directly in my eyes. "Please, do it quickly?"

Still reeling from the shock of knowing I would have to let Finlay go, I nodded to Pen and gently squeezed her hand. "I promise, I won't make you stay."

"Thank you, Soul Keeper," Pen said with quiet reverence.

My mind was filled with thoughts of losing everyone who mattered to me when an awful thought suddenly struck me.

"Pen?"

"Mmm." Her voice had started to soften and her eyes had taken on a faraway look.

"If Finlay is already lost, am I supposed to stop the veil from being torn down by sending his soul on now?"

Pen seemed to become lucid again, just long enough to say, "Flora, I cannot force you to decide either way. Everything that has happened has come down to this moment, and right or wrong it has fallen onto your young shoulders to make the decision for all of us."

"I'm afraid, Pen," I confessed. "I don't want to lose anyone."

"I trust you, Flora. You will make the right choices, and you will save us all. I love you, sweetheart."

I bowed my head. "Thank you, Pen. I love you too."

When she didn't reply, I lifted my head, and the tears that had been threatening for so long, finally spilled over and onto my cheeks as I realised that Pen was no longer here.

After an age, I stood up and gently kissed Pen's forehead before slipping out of the room and closing the door behind me.

I looked down at Finlay's sleeping form, envying his blissful unawareness, when suddenly my eyes landed on a tiny patch of discoloured skin that peeked out from beneath the cuff of his long-sleeved top.

I reached down and hooked the grey material with my index finger. As I pulled it gently back to reveal a large patch of skin that looked twisted and burnt, I bit my lip in horror.

The Super's body was rejecting him.

"Hi, Flor." He suddenly opened his unfamiliar eyes and stared up at me. That was when I really let myself fall apart.

CHAPTER 21

Finlay and I sat in the hospital corridor and held each other for what felt like hours. I wasn't entirely sure who took the most comfort from the other's embrace. Pen had been like a mother to me, but she had been everything to my best friend.

"She was my mentor, my mother, and my friend," he whispered as we sat on the uncomfortable hospital chairs. We still hadn't told the others, and I felt a stab of guilt.

"We have to go back to the terminal, Finlay," I murmured gently. "The other Dion need to know."

He stood up and tried to pull himself together. "I know. I just needed some time first."

I stood up alongside him and hugged him again, but he pulled back from me a little before speaking. "You saw it didn't you?"

I tried to act as though I had no idea what he meant. "Saw what?"

He raised a brow at me. "I felt you pull my sleeve back

before I opened my eyes, Flor. You know, don't you?"

I dropped my eyes to the floor, not ready to shed more tears. "I'm so sorry, Finlay."

"It's all right, Flor. I've had some time to get used to it." He tried to sound brave.

We began walking along the corridor of the hospital. I felt a pang of guilt at leaving Pen all alone, but we couldn't do anything until the hospital agreed to release her body for burial.

Finlay glanced back over his shoulder. "We'll be back for her soon, Flor."

"I know. I just hate leaving her by herself."

He twined his fingers through mine and reassuringly squeezed my hand as we walked out into the warm night air.

"I'm sorry I hid it from you, Flor."

"You hid it because you know how much it hurts me to think of losing you." I tried to sound stronger than I felt. My emotions were teetering on the brink of madness after everything that had happened.

"I know this is a lot to ask, Flor, but you need to be strong now. The other Dion will look to you to lead the way against Sluag." Finlay opened the car door and climbed into the driver seat as he spoke.

"I know. We all have to sit down and talk about what happens next, Finlay." I made my decision then. "But, I need to talk with you and Lyall alone first."

Arriving back at the terminal was one of the hardest moments of my life since finding out that my parents had died.

I felt like an angel of death, bringing news that shattered the hearts of my Dion and tore down the last remaining hope they had that we could take Sluag down.

When the things I wanted to say to reassure them just wouldn't come and I thought they would fall apart in the same way as me, I was once again thankful for the one person on whom I could always rely.

"Tonight, we will grieve. We will remember Pen and celebrate an incredible woman, who devoted her life to two Soul Keepers. Tomorrow, we will bury her with honour, and the day after we will carry on her legacy by laying our plans to destroy Sluag and save the goddamn world."

When Lyall finished speaking, I breathed out a sigh of relief. I had never met anyone stronger and braver and more suited to standing up to Sluag.

Freya smiled through her tears. "She was an incredible woman."

Artair raised a glass of water he had been holding in trembling fingers. "To Penthesilea, one of the greatest Dion to ever live."

"To Pen," Bear echoed him.

Finlay had crossed the room until he was standing close enough behind me to whisper in my ear so no one else could hear. "If there was ever any doubt in my mind as to why you chose Lyall, he just one hundred percent proved it. He's the best of all of us, Flor."

My lip quivered in shame as I wondered for the thousandth

time, how I could let Lyall get closer to dying with every moment that passed without my intervention.

I swallowed back my guilt and answered Finlay back. "There's somewhere I have to be. Do you want to come?"

He gave me a questioning look. "Where?"

I started toward the door, and he followed me outside. "I have a promise to keep," I said quietly.

Realisation dawned in Finlay's eyes as I started to fade into the Everwood. He followed after me quickly, and we both appeared beneath the Síorraidh trees.

"Do you really need to do this now, Flor?" His voice was tense.

A bright white light—almost identical to Finlay in soul form—floated through the trees and sedately hovered to a stop in front of my best friend.

Yes, she does because I asked it of her, Finlay.

Tears sprang to his eyes as Pen's voice sounded inside our heads.

"Pen, I'm so sorry. We should have done more." Finlay's voice was cracked and broken.

The fiercely white light bobbed toward Finlay's face and grazed gently past his cheek.

It was my time, sunshine. She used the name she hadn't called him since he was a little boy. *I'm ready to go on, and we all know that I'll be back.*

"But, you won't remember us," he whispered.

I'll never forget you. How could I? She spoke in a whisper inside our minds.

Finlay nodded sadly as the little white light floated toward me and stopped just level with my chest.

It's time, Soul Keeper.

More tears burned behind my eyes. *Would I ever stop crying again?* "Are you sure, Pen? You can wait until your memories fade."

The beautifully bright orb swayed gently in the air before me.

I want to remember everything. I'm sure.

"Okay," I whispered.

I knew this had to be different from any other soul sorting, and instinctively I dropped to my knees and bowed my head reverently. Finlay did the same, and I started to speak the words that came easily to my mind.

"Penthesilea Michaelson, you are one of the greatest Dion to ever serve our cause. You protected two Soul Keepers in your lifetime, and you were a fierce and formidable warrior in the fight to stop The Host of the Unforgiven Dead from destroying the mortal world."

I took a deep breath to steady my voice before continuing.

"Your time here in this world is done. This version of you will be granted the freedom of peace, but your soul will live on again in the mortal world. Thank you for everything." My voice trailed off to a whisper.

Thank you, Flora.

Pen's voice whispered through my mind, and I raised my

head to allow myself one last glimpse of her face. Finlay did the same, and we both sat back on our knees with matching looks of awe mixing with the tears on our faces as a white-furred tiger turned golden eyes upon us and nodded her head in farewell before bounding into the woods.

CHAPTER

22

When we got back to the terminal, Lyall was angry. I wasn't surprised; I had expected them all to resent not having the opportunity to say farewell.

"Not even a chance to say goodbye, Flora. Jesus, why?" Lyall and I were the only ones left in the main room. The others had headed to bed, mainly, I thought, to give Lyall and me some space.

"Because that's what Pen wanted. She's bloody dead, Lyall. I owed her a last wish," I snapped.

He stood with his hands rested flat on the opposite side of the table from where I sat. His voice was quieter now. "What's wrong with you these days, love? You keep pushing everyone away and keeping secrets from us."

"I don't push everyone away," I murmured stubbornly.

"Everyone except Finlay, then." He spoke quietly now, but that didn't take the sting out of his words.

"And here we are, again. I'm going to bed, Lyall. We have a

Dion to bury tomorrow." I crossed the room and slammed my bedroom door closed behind me.

Why do we push away the people we love the most? I wondered to myself as I lay back in the uncomfortable bed.

I already knew why I was pushing Lyall away. I couldn't stand the thought of losing him, and I was trying to distance myself to protect my heart from breaking more than it already had.

After hours of restless tossing and turning, I finally fell asleep, but not in to the blissful unconsciousness I had hoped for.

I knew I was dreaming, and it wasn't a Summoning. This was just my own mind reminding me of exactly what lay ahead of us all.

My Dion and I were in the grounds of Castle Dion. Sluag had made the castle his home since escaping the Endwood, and so it had become the place where we would make our final stand against him.

We had an impressive army that was at least two hundred Draugur strong. Sluag had less Draugur, but his Super Draugur numbers were significantly higher than I had last calculated them to be. I glanced frantically at my Dion, but each of them was there—except Pen of course.

How did he have so many Supers?

Sluag raised a scaly arm and signalled his Draugur to attack. We sent our own army forward to meet them, and the two forces clashed together like the waves of a storm-torn sea.

All of my Dion shifted into their animal alters to join in the attack, except for two. Lyall stayed by my side to protect me and to feed me his energy when the time came to get Sluag in the box. Finlay didn't change because his body had been falling apart for days now, and he didn't have the strength to do it.

As Finlay's Super Draugur body suddenly burst apart and ejected the bright, white orb from its chest, I ran toward him as though I could help him somehow.

Falling to my knees next to the husk of the Super Draugur body, I cradled its head in my arms. With horror, I realised that Finlay's soul would be trapped in the mortal world forever.

"Fool." Sluag's contemptuous voice made my head snap up in time to see him grip Lyall by the hair and yank his head back.

"No," I begged.

As a silver blade appeared in Sluag's hand, I looked desperately around me for help, but all of my other Dion were dead or dying on the battlefield. Lyall was the only one left, and I was going to lose him too.

As Sluag drew the blade across Lyall's throat, and the blood started to flow, he bellowed with laughter and triumph. "Bow to me, Flora, for you have lost your war."

"No," I howled. "Never, I won't. No, no, no."

I woke up alone in the darkness. I had been crying out in my sleep, and judging by the state of my bedding, I had been kicking and thrashing too. I reached out blindly and found a glass of water by the side of my bed and drank it back in two deep swallows.

I smoothed my hair back from my sweat-soaked forehead and swung my legs out of the bed. I sat on the edge of the bed for ten minutes to allow my breathing to slow and my heart to stop racing.

I needed comfort, and I knew where to get it. Crossing the bedroom, I opened my door and crept out into the main room. Lyall was still sitting at the table. It hurt my heart to see him sitting there alone. He looked so desolate. I walked up behind him, laid my head against his shoulders, and wrapped my arms around his neck.

He stiffened for a second and then relaxed as he brought his hand up to hold on to mine.

"I'm sorry," I whispered.

"Me too." Without warning, he grabbed my arms and pulled me around until I was folded in his arms and sat on his knee.

"Whoa, I need to apologise more often." I laughed.

He buried his face against my hair and whispered, "Now isn't the time to fight, love. We need a united front."

"I know," I murmured, enjoying the warmth and security of his arms.

"But we have to be honest, Flora. No secrets." His words made me shiver, despite the warmth of him.

"Then there are things that I need to tell you," I confessed.

He nodded as though it was what he had expected. "Tell me, love."

I hesitated. "Finlay needs to be here too."

He was silent for a moment before nodding once. "Okay, then we'll get some more sleep, and the three of us will talk in the morning."

"What about the hospital?" I asked.

"We'll send Bear and Artair to collect Pen. We can talk while they're away, and then we will lay her to rest in the afternoon."

I bit my lip. "I wish we could bury her at Castle Dion."

It was customary that all fallen Dion be buried at the Castle, in a tiny cemetery that was walled on three sides and was bordered by the shore of Loch Ness on the fourth.

We wouldn't have the chance to bury Pen there as long as the castle was occupied by Draugur.

"I know. It's too dangerous, though, love. Pen would understand." He shifted in his chair and we both stood up. I realised I was exhausted—a common feeling for me these days.

"I don't want to bury her in this place, Lyall. It's dark and dingy and ramshackle. It's nothing like how she was in life." My voice was firm.

"There's a grove of willows on this side of the loch. It's about two miles from here, which means it sits directly opposite Castle Dion. I thought it might be the next best place for her." He had obviously thought this through.

"Thank you, not just for the willows but for the speech you gave earlier and for the way you always take care of me." I leaned up and kissed him gently on the cheek.

He captured my face with his hands and leaned down to

kiss my forehead in the usual place. "I'll always take care of you, love. For as long as there's breath in my body."

I shuddered at his last sentence as I remembered back to my dream.

"Flora, are you all right?" He sounded worried.

"As long as you still have breath in your body, yes," I quipped.

"What?"

"Never mind, I'm tired. I'll be fine after I get some sleep." I waved off his concern.

As we returned to bed, I hoped that what I had said was the truth.

CHAPTER
23

Breakfast the next morning was miserable. Whether or not it was consciously done, we had left the seat at the head of the table empty, and I noticed all of the others glancing at it sadly from time to time.

Lyall instructed Bear and Artair to collect Pen. When Enid and Freya asked if they could go too, I was relieved when Lyall agreed. That meant we had the terminal to ourselves, and I could be completely honest without having to worry about being overheard.

I suspected we would tell the others everything soon, but for now, it was going to be tough enough to tell Finlay and Lyall they were destined to die.

After the other Dion had left, we sat at the table in the dismal light of the main terminal room, and I related everything to them both. I started with what Eric had told me when he handed over the box, and I ended with my dream the night before.

"I have no idea how much of my dream is true. But, it felt like a warning of what was going to happen and it was awful," I admitted.

Lyall and Finlay were both quiet for a moment while they seemed to think over everything I had told them. Finlay was the first to break the silence.

"Flor, you have to obliterate my soul. If doing that kills the Supers, then the veil will hold and no one else has to die."

"I'm not obliterating you, Finlay. I won't do it," I hissed.

Support came from an unexpected quarter. "There's no chance on earth we're sending your soul into oblivion, Finlay. No one deserves that. Especially not a Dion," Lyall said quietly.

Finlay persisted. "Think about this for a minute. If that veil drops then you're gonna die, Lyall."

I flinched as though I had been slapped.

Finlay didn't stop there, however. "It may not only be Lyall who dies, Flor. What about Artair? Freya? You? That's before we talk about how many innocent people Sluag will kill before we stop him."

I folded my arms tightly over my chest. "This was why I didn't want to tell you. I knew you'd both be fighting to get yourselves killed."

Lyall shrugged. "Not me, love. I have no intention of getting killed when we put Sluag in that box."

I almost screamed in frustration. "Argh, you don't get it. I've seen what the end looks like, Lyall, and it's hideous. You can't avoid it if you're there, so you have to stay away."

Lyall laughed out loud. "What sort of Dion—No, what sort of bonded Dion would I be if I went into hiding while my Soul Keeper was fighting for her life? No chance. Non-negotiable, love."

Finlay spoke more quietly and more reasonably. "Lyall, she's right. You need to stay away." Lyall started to argue, but Finlay calmly raised a hand and carried on talking.

"Pen's gone, I'll be gone before much longer, and Flora will need you. I can't stop what's gonna happen to me. Whether Flor obliterates me, or whether this body kicks me out, I can't be Finlay anymore. She needs you, Lyall, now more than ever."

I'd never heard Finlay sound so mature and so selfless, not in all of the years I had known him. In that moment, I understood that perhaps in another world and another time, I might have loved him in the way that he loved me.

Lyall didn't seem about to back down, however. "Let's look at this another way?"

"What other way is there?" I asked.

"If Finlay is truly the key to stopping Sluag, then if you obliterate him, there's never going to be any coming back from that." Lyall clasped his hands together and leaned over the table.

"But if I'm gone, the Supers will die with me and the veil won't fall." Finlay spoke matter-of-factly.

Lyall spread his hands in a "fair play" gesture before continuing. "Then what happens if in, say ten years, Sluag bags himself a new Dion and creates more Supers? What if you still should have been the *one* to defeat him but you're gone? The world will fall anyway."

I raised my eyebrows. "I hadn't thought of it like that. But, Lyall's right, Finlay. We can't take the chance that we might still need you down the line."

"This is ridiculous," Finlay complained. "Flora, I know I can't make you destroy me but I'm begging you, both of you." He looked at Lyall as he finished speaking.

Lyall shook his head. "Sorry, no can do. The Soul Keeper has spoken."

I quickly shifted my attention to Lyall. "You're not off the hook yet. If you don't come with us to Castle Dion, you won't die, and I can't let you die, Lyall."

He narrowed his eyes at me. "You know as well as I do, if you don't have me there to share my energy with you, then you can't kick Sluag out of his body, Flora. You've got no choice but to keep me by your side, love. Until the bitter end."

He was right. I didn't know if I would be able to box Sluag, even with Lyall's energy. Without it, I was certain I wouldn't manage it. When I didn't say anything, Lyall grinned in triumph.

"You need me there, love, and you know it."

I shook my head sadly as I studied the determination in both of their faces. This was what true loyalty looked like. I felt a storm of conflicting emotions warring within my body.

I was terrified I would lose one or both of them in the coming fight with Sluag, but I was also touched and humbled by how fiercely committed to their cause these two were. I was sure I was the most fortunate Soul Keeper in history.

"All right," I whispered.

"All right what?" Finlay asked.

"If I can't negotiate with either of you, then things will just have to happen the way that fate directs them. I refuse to obliterate my best friend, Finlay, and I know I can't keep you from the fight, Lyall." I shrugged. There was nothing else I could do.

"So, we'll work together to come up with a strategy that ensures we get Sluag into that box." Lyall spoke with more confidence than I felt.

"I just hope we don't end up unleashing hell on the world in the meantime," I said quietly.

Lyall reached out and put a comforting hand over mine. "I'm not gonna let that happen, love. We have everything we need to take Sluag down, and we're not going to stop until we do."

I breathed out a sigh of relief. I had been so afraid to tell them the truth, and now that I had, I only wished I'd done it sooner.

The sound of a car pulling up to the front of the terminal made us all turn toward the door. I held my breath, unsure if I was ready to face seeing Pen's body again, or the impending funeral.

The door burst open and a white-faced Artair was the first person to appear.

Obviously sensing something was majorly wrong, Lyall jumped up from his seat. "Artair, what is it, mate?"

The other three Dion were inside the main room by now, and each looked as shocked as Artair.

Artair sat down heavily at the table and turned haunted eyes on Lyall. "She's gone, Lyall. Pen's body is gone."

I blinked slowly before speaking. "What do you mean, gone?"

"He means gone, Flora. She's been taken, and I'll give you one guess, who by?" Freya's eyes were wide.

"Sluag," Finlay growled.

"But why would he take her when she's already dead?" Enid asked quietly.

"To torment us?" Freya suggested.

I thought back to my dream, remembering my confusion at the new Supers in Sluag's army. I hadn't understood where he'd got them all from.

Now I did. "No, not to torment us. He's going to use her blood to create more Supers and bring down the veil."

CHAPTER
24

"Shit." Finlay punched the table as he shouted.

"We should never have left her alone." I shook my head angrily.

How could we have been so stupid?

Before anyone could speak another word, Finlay darted through the open door and disappeared. It was obvious where he was headed.

"Lyall, we have to stop him." I ran toward the door, and I heard Lyall break into a jog behind me.

"The rest of you stay here in case Sluag has discovered the terminal," he called back over his shoulder.

Lyall and I materialised in the Everwood and didn't hesitate, instead breaking into a run for the boundary line. Finlay was nowhere to be seen, but there was a trail of pure souls that followed us along the path, and I could hear them talking at me animatedly inside my head.

Finlay was here, Flora. He's going to the Endwood. He'll

be killed.

Again, I thought grimly.

We managed to gain some ground on Finlay, and we came running down the slope toward the boundary just in time to see him stop at the line and roar, "Sluag. Come here, now."

"Finlay, enough," Lyall snapped as he approached the boundary line warily."

"No, Lyall," Finlay hissed. "Pen deserves better than this. He's gone too far this time."

"Have I, traitor?" Sluag's voice rang across the border. "What exactly do you propose to do about it?"

"Give her back, Sluag?" I levelled my cool gaze on his scaly, grey features.

"I might, once she's been entirely drained of blood, Little Dreamer." He spoke matter-of-factly.

Finlay took a step closer to the Endwood. "I'm going to kill you for this, Sluag."

A slow grin stretched across Sluag's hideous face as he raised an arm and crooked his index finger in Finlay's direction. "Well come on then, traitor. Have at it."

With a roar of complete rage, Finlay launched himself across the boundary toward Sluag, and with a cold stab of fear, I realised I was too far away to intervene.

Suddenly, a black shadow appeared from nowhere and leapt across the border to crash into Finlay, sending him reeling back into the Everwood.

My relief at Lyall's intervention was short-lived as I

KATE KEIR

realised my wolf was still inside the Endwood, and two Supers were rapidly closing the distance between him and them.

"Lyall, run," I screamed as he turned a full circle and leapt for the safety of the border.

The first Super leaned out and grabbed hold of Lyall's back paw, bringing him crashing to the ground halfway across the border. The second Draugur caught up seconds later and slipped a knife from its wide sleeve.

"No," I shouted as I ran toward them.

"No," Sluag's voice boomed, and the Supers both became as still as statues. The one holding Lyall's paw, released its grip, enabling Lyall to scramble to his feet and drag himself across the boundary, back into the Everwood. He was panting heavily but unharmed.

I looked at Sluag questioningly, and whether it was because of our supposed "bond" or whether he just understood what I was asking, he answered me.

"I don't want Lyall dead, Flora. You know I would much prefer to have him sit at my right hand." Sluag lifted his right hand up and pretended to study it.

Never going to happen. Lyall's voice growled inside my head.

Without thinking, I reached down and gently touched my hand to the top of the great wolf's head. He reached out with his huge tongue and licked me.

I nodded to Lyall and crossed the grass until I was standing next to Finlay—he was standing and glaring at Sluag, unmoving.

151

I wrapped my arm through his and whispered in his ear. "I need you alive, Finlay. You can't take risks like that again."

Sluag clearly had superb hearing. "That abomination, on the other hand." He pointed to Finlay as he spoke. "I would kill him in a heartbeat."

I felt Finlay tense beneath my hand, and my own anger sparked again. "Abomination? He's only become what you've made him, Sluag."

Sluag snorted. "I didn't make Finlay what he is, you did, Flora. You swap him from body to body for your own selfish gain. Did you ever stop to ask what Finlay wanted?"

I shot a guilt-ridden glance at my best friend, trapped inside the body of a man twice his own age. Finlay's eyes had a haunted look. He had lost everything in the fight to stop Sluag, including the woman he considered a mother. It was no wonder he was such a mess.

"I'm sorry it has to be this way," I whispered.

Finlay shifted slightly, pulling his arm out of mine. I tensed, expecting him to attack Sluag again. Instead, I felt him twine his fingers through mine and take a deep breath.

Facing Sluag, Finlay spoke calmly. "I'm not sorry, Flora. Not if it means that when the end comes, I will be a part of finishing this *abomination*"—he spat the word back at Sluag— "forever. Once he's inside that box, then I can move on, and I'll be happy to do it."

Sluag mockingly placed a hand over where his heart would have been—if he actually had one.

"Ah, so very touching, Finlay. Doesn't bring Penthesilea back, though, does it?"

Next to me, Finlay flinched as though he had been slapped. I narrowed my eyes at Sluag but tried to speak calmly through my rage.

"Okay, I get that you're not going to give Pen back until you have what you want. But, once you have her blood, there's nothing stopping you from letting us have her back to be buried."

He cocked a tufted grey brow at me. "So, calm and rational, Little Dreamer. It is almost as though I were talking with Penthesilea herself."

I took a step forward, not taking my own eyes off the burning pits of Sluag's.

"Please, Sluag. Treat her with the honour and respect that she deserves."

He was silent for a very long time. He looked first at me and then to Finlay, who stood pale and silent beside me. Finally, his gaze shifted to Lyall, who stood a few feet away from us, still in wolf form.

Lyall's lips peeled back in the tiniest hint of a snarl as Sluag studied him.

Lyall, I warned inside my head. He stopped instantly, instead simply levelling his amber glare on Sluag's face.

After what felt like an eternity, Sluag spoke.

"No," was all he said.

My eyes widened with anger. "What? Why?"

Sluag slowly shook his hideous head from side to side.

"Because, I'm the bad guy in this story, Flora. I have no idea as to what would make you think I would show any kindness to a Soul Keeper or one of her Dion. Especially the Soul Keeper who is predicted to be my downfall."

I raised a brow at that. *So, he knew I was destined to finish him.*

He was still speaking. "I'm quite certain that my Draugur will have finished exsanguinating Penthesilea's body by now, and once I am certain that we have every drop we can take, I will burn her into ashes."

He turned his back on us and started to walk away, deeper in to the Endwood.

"No, Flora. Once I am finished, there will be nothing left of your precious Penthesilea and now that I have her blood, in a matter of days, I will have a whole new army of Super Draugur. I don't think that veil will be up for very much longer, do you?"

The three of us stood and stared at the retreating figure of Sluag. We didn't move until he had completely disappeared amongst the blackened trees.

Once we could no longer see the tall, grey spectre of him, we slowly turned and started to make our way back through the Everwood to the terminal. None of us spoke. I was sure that each of us was wondering just how we were going to tell the others that we would never be able to lay Pen to rest.

CHAPTER
25

All three of us had bowed heads when we arrived back at the terminal. Lyall slunk off to shift back in to human form, and Finlay and I sat down to tell the others what had happened.

"I'm sorry, I shouldn't have lost it like that," Finlay said quietly.

"No one can blame you, Finlay. You were the closest to Pen out of all of us," Freya said softly.

"I hate to shift the focus from Pen right now, but we have a matter of days until the veil falls apart and the world starts to end." Artair frowned.

"He's right," Lyall said as he walked back into the room and sat down next to me. "In fact, we might only have hours."

"What do you mean?" Enid's eyes were wide with worry.

Lyall rested his elbows on the rickety table as he continued. "The veil is fragile. None of us, not even Sluag, know how many more Supers it's going to take to bring it down. He might only need to create one more, and you can bet your ass he's got people working on it as we speak."

Bear spoke up. "So, we still can't kill a Super, and we're gonna be overrun with them in a few days. Do you guys not think that perhaps we're completely screwed?"

"Shut up," Freya hissed.

"Is there any way Flora can eject the Supers' souls, like she did with the pet's for Finlay?" Enid asked.

Lyall spoke gently, as he always did with Enid. He still thought of her as so much younger than she was. "The problem is, Flora had mine and Finlay's help to do that, and it still nearly killed her. We can't do it for all of the Supers Sluag has lined up."

"If we get Sluag's soul in the box, then maybe the Supers will stop following his orders anyway?" Artair shrugged.

"I don't think we should be relying on maybes." Finlay frowned.

"Problem is, maybe might be all we have. We're on the clock now, and at some point soon, we're gonna have to react, no matter how prepared we are," Lyall said calmly.

Enid said what we were all thinking. "What if we lose?"

"I don't expect we'll know all that much about it. We'll be dead," Freya was as tactful as ever as she lounged back in her chair like she didn't have a care in the world.

"Losing isn't an option. I'm not giving the mortal world to Sluag." I spoke firmly.

"Then we need a plan and it needs to work," Artair said.

Finlay spoke up. "I've just had a thought. Would it be possible for me to try and help you push Sluag's soul out of his body, Flor?"

"You mean the same way we kicked the Super out of its body for you?" Lyall asked.

"Yeah." Finlay nodded.

I frowned. "That means you'll have to leave your current body."

Finlay smiled ruefully and held up his arm. As the sleeve fell back to expose the damaged and twisted skin underneath it, the others gasped in shock.

"It's not like this body's gonna let me stay too much longer anyway, Flor."

"The more help we have with this, the better chance we have of getting Sluag in that box, love," Lyall said gently, as though he were speaking to a child and it infuriated me.

I shook my head. "And after it's done, then what happens?"

Finlay gave me a sad smile. "Then you help me to move on, Flor."

Bear's voice broke through the tide of sadness that washed over me. "That still doesn't help us decide what to do with the Supers."

"More Draugur, loyal to Flora, showed up through the night. We now have maybe two hundred of them. Could they each take a Super hostage for us once Sluag is boxed?" Freya suggested.

"It might work, although I imagine Supers are stronger than ordinary Draugur." Artair looked to Lyall for agreement, and I felt a rush of warmth at how my Dion followed his lead so easily.

"They might buy us enough time to get the Supers into spelled cells. We're going to need bigger cells than the ones at Castle Dion to hold them all, though." Lyall looked thoughtful.

"I can contact Eric at the library and find out the exact details of the spell so we can create new holding cells," Enid offered.

"Thank you, Enid, that would be helpful." I smiled gratefully at her.

"I guess we just need to iron out the finer points now then, huh?" Finlay grinned. He was trying to be brave, and it made me both sad and angry in equal parts.

"Realistically, it would make sense to take the fight to Sluag before the veil falls." Bear was surprisingly serious tonight.

I raised a brow. "Fight him in the Endwood?"

"There's logic in that, love. What's the point in waiting for him to create more Draugur and break down the veil?" Lyall nodded his approval at Bear.

"Makes sense to me. The sooner we put that dog down, the better," Finlay agreed.

"Hey, less of the dog," Lyall growled jokingly.

"Wait a minute." I stood up as I spoke.

Everyone looked to me, sensing I wasn't about to agree with the plan.

"Finlay, if you leave your body in the Endwood, then your soul will be trapped there, forever." My voice trembled.

He lowered his eyes to the tabletop as he replied. "What

other choice do we have, Flor? If the veil comes down, hundreds of innocent people could die, maybe more. This is a much better way."

"Better for who?" My voice had increased in pitch.

"Better for all of the people who won't die, Flora." Finlay stared at me through unfamiliar eyes, set within a stranger's face.

"No. We won't take the fight to Sluag in the Endwood. I won't let you give up the chance to come back to the mortal world again, Finlay." I folded my arms over my chest in defiance.

"Then perhaps we need to have a vote on it, Flor." Finlay gazed around the room at the others as he spoke.

I bit my lip as I tried to weigh up how the others would decide to vote. "All right," I managed.

Finlay nodded and stood up. "All those in favour of waiting for the veil to fall?"

I put up my hand alongside Enid. *Two of us. Only two?*

"All those in favour of taking the fight to the Endwood?" Finlay raised his own hand as he spoke.

Four other hands went up alongside Finlay's. When I met Lyall's gaze and looked to his raised hand, I shook my head in despair.

"He's already given up too much," I whispered.

"It's a Dion's job, love. Don't you remember what we told you when you first arrived. We will do anything to protect you and the mortals in your care. If that includes dying, then so be it," Lyall said reverently.

"He's already dead, Lyall. He's going to give his soul to the Endwood." I turned my attention to Finlay. "You once told me you would go mad if you had to spend eternity as a soul. Now you're volunteering to do exactly that but in hell."

Finlay shrugged. "I'd do anything for you, Flor, including saving the world."

"Then it's agreed," Artair said quickly.

"I'll get the spell from Eric and cast it on some new cells for our Super Draugur." Enid stood up quickly, eager to escape the atmosphere at the table, I suspected.

"I think we need to get a rough idea of just how many Supers Sluag has right now," Lyall mused aloud.

"How can we find out?" Freya quizzed.

"Well, if Artair's up for it, I reckon it's time to go and do a little spying in the Endwood." Lyall grinned.

"Let's do it." Artair returned Lyall's smile.

Enid's eyes widened as she placed a hand on Artair's arm. "Be careful."

Bear waggled his eyebrows at Freya. "Looks like me and you need to crack on with some battle training, hotness."

Freya smiled grimly. "Hmm getting to knock you on your ass sounds like my kind of training."

"Oh, you are welcome to keep on trying, babe." Bear winked and smiled at her.

Lyall crossed the room and placed a gentle kiss on my forehead. I tried to stay angry, but it was impossible. "Please, be careful out there."

"I will." He pulled back from me and stared at me with his wolf eyes. "I'm sorry it's not how you wanted it to be, love. But, you know we made the right decision."

"I know," I mumbled.

Lyall lifted his head and looked around at the other Dion. "We don't have much time. I think we probably need to attack within twenty-four hours if we have any chance of stopping the veil from falling."

Everyone nodded their agreement, and I felt my heart turn to ice as I stared at each of them in turn. In the space of just one day, I could lose every single Dion in this room and also my own life.

CHAPTER
26

Bear and Freya asked me if I wanted to join them for battle training. Finlay was going along with them too, and Enid had promised to catch them up as soon as she had spelled the underground bunker at the terminal, ready for our Super hostages.

I had tried to reason with Lyall that Freya would make a better spy, since Sluag had promised not to harm her when she was in raven form and escorting rogues to the Endwood.

Lyall had stood his ground, insisting that "all bets were now off" and that Sluag would tear Freya apart if he caught her. I had quickly realised that Lyall was right, and Sluag didn't care about his supply of rogues any longer. He had zero intention of staying inside the Endwood anyway.

I politely refused to train with the other Dion. There wasn't any real point in me honing my battle skills—Lyall wouldn't let me get near enough to the action to join in. But, apart from that, I had a responsibility to stay at the side lines and work on parting

Sluag's soul from his hideous body.

I wondered, not for the first time, why Sluag chose such a repulsive body to inhabit. I remembered back to when I had first encountered The Host of the Unforgiven Dead, and he had taken the face of my father. He could appear in any form he wanted, yet he chose to be a scaly, grey demon.

In reality, he likely wanted to appear as terrifying as he possibly could. I smiled weakly to myself; his image was a cliché, just like so many other things in my crazy, messed up, Soul Keeper's world.

I had suddenly been overwhelmed by a desperate desire to go home, one last time. I wanted to see my little cottage—my last link to my parents and to Achilles. When I asked Lyall whether he thought it was a really stupid idea, he hadn't been dead against it.

"I very much doubt Sluag will suspect you're gonna go home for a visit under the circumstances, love. It's quite possibly the safest place you could be right now. Just be careful, okay?"

I had promised I would be, so when he and Artair set off to find a discreet way to hop over the border between the Everwood and the Endwood, I had struck out for home by myself.

I slowly walked up the seventeen steps that were cut into the hillside that led to the front door of the cottage. It was a beautiful day and although the garden was now neglected and overgrown, it was still like standing in a little corner of paradise, especially after so long spent living in the darkness of the terminal.

When I got to the door, I took a deep breath and gently rested my forehead against the oak-coloured wood. My mind went back to a time when I was happy here, living with my parents and Achilles. Once upon a thousand years ago, I had been an ordinary girl, who just seemed to get recognised a lot more often than anyone should.

"I miss you so much," I whispered aloud, not sure if I was talking to my parents or my life before all this. I turned the key in the lock and let the door swing open.

Inside the cottage was cool, as only a two-hundred-year-old building can be in the summer. The front door led directly in to the kitchen in the way that so many old houses in Scotland did. I looked up at the familiar wooden beams that criss-crossed the ceiling.

Cobwebs stretched elegantly from beam to beam, gossamer strands that glinted with gold as they caught the shafts of sunlight which filtered through the tiny kitchen windows. I heard a scuttling sound and realised that mice had probably moved in to the warm and quiet building in my absence.

Something glinted in the corner of my eye, and as I turned toward the sideboard by the front door, I noticed the knife that I had held in my shaky hand to greet Finlay on the night I had first *really* seen Castle Dion.

I picked up the knife and examined it, remembering every detail of what came after Finlay had taken it from me. The moment he stilled my fear by wrapping me in the comfort of a bear hug. Then the drive to Loch Ness and the boat journey

164

through the moonlit water, until we eventually found Pen waiting for us on the shore.

I choked back tears as I thought of Pen and dropped the knife back onto the sideboard before stepping through the kitchen and into the living room, which was like a shrine to my past life. I walked past pictures fixed to the wall that showed my parents and me out on our boat, walking in the woods, and even just relaxing in the garden.

I noticed a grumpy Achilles in the background of one picture and felt a wave of guilt rush over me. I should have at least gone back to the castle to look for him and Phobos and Deimos. They could be anywhere now, maybe cold and hungry. I just hoped that they had stuck together so that they at least had each other.

A sudden scraping sound behind me made me whirl around, bringing me face to face with Sluag. I choked on the words I tried to speak, because I was so unused to seeing him in an environment outside the Endwood. Standing inside my living room, he looked tall and terrifying and ancient.

"Hello, Little Dreamer." He grinned blackly.

I looked over his shoulder, toward the kitchen, desperately wishing I hadn't put the knife back down. "How are you here?" I finally managed to ask.

"I'm not really here, Flora. At least not yet." He crossed the room and sat down on my parents' country-style sofa, and a confused giggle erupted from my mouth.

"What's funny, Flora?" He gave me a crooked smile, like

someone who was trying to be nice to a child they didn't particularly want to talk to.

"Seeing you here, in my house, on my sofa. It's just, really weird," I confessed.

He surveyed the room before replying. "I suppose it does feel a little strange, doesn't it?"

I sobered suddenly. "Why haven't you killed me yet?"

He sighed dramatically. "Because, much as I would like to, I can't, Little Dreamer."

"Why not?" Internally, I sagged with relief at his confession.

"Like I said, I'm not really here, Flora. You see, when I created my latest Super Draugur, using Penthesilea's blood, the veil tore a little more. That has allowed me to project myself into the mortal world. But, I can't actually do anything here yet."

As if to prove his point, he reached out and swiped at a vase on the table next to the sofa, and his hand glided straight through it.

I frowned with worry. If the veil had torn enough to let Sluag project himself here, then it wouldn't be much longer before he could really enter the mortal world.

He noticed my concern and grinned. "Yes, it won't be long now, Little Dreamer, and you and your dammed Dion will be the very first on my list of people to murder."

"If I were to let you kill me before the veil drops, would you leave the others alone?" I asked him seriously.

"So self-sacrificing, Flora. But, no, I wouldn't. I want to

watch each and every one of you burn." He smirked. "Just as Penthesilea did."

"Honestly, Sluag, we are going to stop you. I might lose one or more of my Dion doing it. I might die myself. But, you're going in to that box, even if I have to put you in there with the last breath in my body."

"What if you have to put me in there with the last breath in Lyall's body, Little Dreamer?" He studied me closely.

"Then I'll do it," I lied.

He sniggered. "No, you won't, Flora."

I didn't trust myself to reply, so I stayed quiet.

He stood up quickly. "Well, as much as I would like to stay and chat in your delightful home, I have to get back and check on the progress of my Super Draugur army."

I stayed silent, staring at his cloaked back until he reached the doorway. "Sluag?" I finally called.

He turned around to look at me, and his eyes burned with an intensity I hadn't seen before. He was terrifying. I swallowed hard but I stood my ground and spoke calmly and quietly.

"I'm going to destroy you. I know you think I'm a stupid child and that I have too many loyalties and too many people who I care about, to be strong enough to do what I need to when the end comes. But, those loyalties and those people, are the reason I *will* win this war."

He gave a soft laugh. "Flora, each and every one of you is as good as dead, but I admire your courage. I confess, you have been my favourite of all of the Soul Keepers that have ever been, and in a hall of fame that houses thousands, you should remain content with that."

"See you on the battlefield." I held my head high as I said it.

"No, Little Dreamer, you'll see me in hell."

CHAPTER 27

It took the length of the entire drive home for me to stop trembling after my encounter with Sluag. Once he left the cottage, I had hastily pulled down the photograph that had captured the image of both my parents and Achilles before locking up and heading for my jeep.

When I got back to the terminal, I sat in the car for another couple of minutes with my head resting on the steering wheel, before I decided to see if I could find the Dion in the Everwood. I didn't want to be by myself right now.

When the Síorraidh trees appeared around me, I instantly relaxed. Nothing could soothe my soul like this place could. I closed my eyes and listened until I picked up the sounds of my Dion, and I set off through the blue-flowered trees.

As I walked, I was approached by hundreds of tiny multi-coloured orbs, each with its own little lightning storm excitedly flickering inside it. They bobbed around me and called my name. The pure souls knew I was more confident now than I had been before, and they worried less about upsetting me. So, they cheekily approached me on their terms, instead of my own.

I laughed in delight as the little lights settled in my hair and along my arms. I could feel the goodness and purity coming off them in waves. It was so much easier to communicate with them now than it had been when I first tried. I didn't need to use my silver net to hold them together anymore. It was as though I could shout loud enough and far enough inside my head that they could all hear me at once.

The rogue souls also knew I was more proficient at being a Soul Keeper and the few that I saw, warily kept their distance. Except for one bright green soul that pulsed with anger and hatred. It pushed its way through the pure souls and darted toward me.

The pure souls scattered apart, trying to avoid touching the rogue. I was furious. I reached out with my right hand and prepared to obliterate it, even though I knew I should preserve every ounce of my energy for the coming fight with Sluag.

Flora Bast, you will die in the war that is to come. Lyall will die and Finlay will be lost forever. Kneel before my master, or know what it is to be destroyed.

"It's you who'll be destroyed," I murmured. Then I lifted my arm again and spoke the words that would erase this little monster for good.

"Esperi rith tai, mortis oct suoil, fortun rais dor, al noi pertina."

The rogue barely got a chance to howl in rage before it

popped and disappeared into oblivion.

My pure souls rallied back around me, and I spoke soothingly to them. "You're okay, it's gone. It can't hurt you now."

Then my ears picked up the noises of the others practising their battle skills, and I hurried on toward the sound.

When I walked into the clearing the Dion were using to practise, I quickly found myself smiling. I knew that Bear and Freya could scrap, but I hadn't been prepared for Enid's ferocity and elegant skill.

She was sparring with Finlay, and although I suspected Finlay was putting everything he had into the exchange, Enid danced on light feet to easily avoid his open hand, time and time again.

I leaned against a tree and watched in silence, enjoying the purity of the moment. This could almost be friends testing each other for fun on a day off from work or college.

Finlay finally lost his temper and rushed at Enid, obviously in an attempt to use his superior strength to knock her off her feet. Enid had other ideas, however, side-stepping my best friend and hooking her toe under his shin to give a swift flick of her foot that spun him around, leaving him to land on his back with a hard thud.

As Finlay panted and gasped, trying to get his breath back, I clapped my hands together in approval and walked toward the group.

"Well done, Enid. That was impressive." I smiled at her.

She blushed furiously. "It was all right. I just got lucky."

I held my hand out to Finlay and helped him up. "No, he got angry and that let you take advantage."

Finlay nodded as he stood up and brushed himself off. "Flor's right, it was my own fault. Nice moves, though, Enid."

Freya touched my elbow gently. "Did you get what you needed at home?"

My voice was grim. "Oh, I got what I needed and a bit more."

She frowned. "What do you mean?"

I told them about my encounter with Sluag. Finlay's face darkened with each word.

"It won't be long now before the veil tears completely," Freya acknowledged.

"Did you spell the terminal?" I asked Enid.

She nodded. "Yep, the entire basement area is spelled to the hilt. Even a Super won't be able to do a thing in there."

"Good work, thanks, Enid." I smiled at her.

She looked as though she wanted to say more, so I encouraged her to carry on.

"Enid, what else?"

"When I spoke with Eric, he told me that a ton of Supers had showed up outside the library. They can't get in, but it's as though they're keeping watch over the place. I told Eric that he and the other librarians needed to stay inside until this was over."

My lips formed a grim line. If we failed in defeating Sluag, so many people were going to die. Losing this fight just wasn't an option.

"It's okay," I reassured her. "They'll back off once Sluag is out of his body."

She gave me a doubtful glance but said nothing.

Freya's voice sounded light. "Why don't you tell Flora, Enid?"

"Tell me what?" I asked inquisitively.

Enid's eyes sparkled as she held out her hand toward me. "It's probably best if I just show you."

For the second time that day, I was suddenly and without warning, dragged back into the past. My mind was filled with the image of Finlay telling me it would be easier if he just showed me Castle Dion, rather than explaining about the first-ever Draugur I encountered.

"Flora?" Enid looked worried as I zoned out.

Snapping back to the present, I gave her a weak smile and took her offered hand. "Sorry. Show me what?"

Enid led me through the trees, and the other Dion followed behind. A group of pure souls gathered around us and bobbed along at a short distance away. I could feel their excitement coming off them in tiny waves, and I wondered exactly what Enid was going to show me.

When Enid finally stopped walking and dropped my hand, I immediately recognised the clearing in which we stood. It was the place where Artair had laid Mara's body so the animal souls could grieve their lost Soul Keeper. My heart ached as I remembered the look on Mara's face as she had died in front of me.

Obviously sensing my sadness, Enid smiled reassuringly. "I didn't bring you here to make you sad, Flora."

"Why are we here?" I asked. I sounded colder than I had meant to.

Enid swept her arm across the clearing in a broad gesture. "Look."

As I followed her instruction, I gasped in surprise. Hundreds of animal souls started to materialise out of the woods and began walking toward us. They were led by a beautiful, brown-eyed deer which I recognised as the same doe who had led the mourning party for Mara.

There were tigers, wolves, bears, snakes, and birds. They weren't solid animals, more like shimmering, ghostly versions of their former selves. They were made up of the same diversity of colours that my human souls were.

Every kind of animal imaginable came to stand before our group. The doe—who was a rich shade of purple—stopped before me and bowed her head slightly in greeting.

"Why are they here, Enid?" I knew she could communicate with them but I could not.

"They want to help," she replied simply.

"How?" I breathed.

"They will fight for us, if we allow it." Enid smiled at the doe, who nodded her head in apparent agreement.

I was confused. "How can they fight for us when they're

trapped here until they reincarnate?"

"This is your kingdom, Flora. Yes, these are my souls, but with your permission they can leave the confines of the Everwood and fight Sluag's Supers and rogues alongside us."

Finlay touched my arm gently. "What do you say, Flor? Your army is starting to look pretty formidable."

I was worried. "Can they be hurt?"

"No," Enid confirmed. "They're still souls so they can't be damaged by Sluag's followers."

I met the doe's brown eyes, and she nodded her head again as if to reassure me that Enid spoke the truth.

"All you need to do is give them your permission, Flor," Finlay encouraged.

I smiled at the doe. "Then you have it. You have my permission and my thanks."

I could feel their delight as they turned and started to retrace their steps back into the Everwood. I watched them, wondering if they would come back.

The doe stayed for a moment longer, and she stepped forward to touch her nose to my hand. As she touched me, I could suddenly hear her voice inside my mind.

Thank you, Flora. When you need us, we will come.

The doe's voice sounded like crystal-clear water cascading down a river in the middle of the most beautiful forest in the world, and it lifted my heart to know that she was fighting for us.

As the doe walked away to follow the other animal souls, I felt a fire rising inside me. Perhaps we might have a chance to win this war after all.

CHAPTER 28

We became less buoyant as we returned to the terminal to find that Lyall and Artair had still not returned from their trip to the Endwood. Freya and Enid used the small kitchen to throw some food together, using the sparse rations that remained, while Finlay and I went down to the basement to investigate Enid's handiwork with the spell.

"How are you holding up, Flor?" His voice was quiet, but I heard him easily in the gloomy stillness of the underground chamber.

"I'm holding up." It was the best I could offer right now.

"For what it's worth, Flor, I am sorry that it has to be this way."

I turned toward the sound of his voice, and I could just make out the shape of his stranger's body in the dim light.

"This might sound really selfish, Finlay, but I envy you in a way," I confessed.

I heard the note of surprise in his voice. "Why?"

I sighed. "Because you have a chance of oblivion, Finlay. Once you're gone and once Lyall is gone, I might still be here, and if that happens, it's going to hurt like hell."

He growled softly, the rumble vibrating through the still air of the basement. "There's no *might* about you still being here, Flor. Your death isn't an option. You're the reason for it all."

I kicked my boot at the bare earthen floor like a moody child. "I know, I have to stay alive or the world burns, I get it. Doesn't mean I have to want to live without you lot around me."

Large hands came out of the darkness and gently but firmly gripped my cheeks. At first, I tensed under the unfamiliar touch but then relaxed, as my mind realised it was just Finlay in his Super body.

"No, Flora. You don't have to stay alive for the rest of the world. Screw the rest of the world."

My mouth dropped open at the desperation in his voice. I started to speak, but he cut me off as he carried on talking in a low and urgent tone.

"You have to stay alive because a world without you in it, isn't a world anyone should have to live in. You're special, Flor. There's something about you that makes everyone who meets you adore you."

"Freya did *not* adore me, when she met me," I countered jokingly.

He didn't hesitate. "And yet she's upstairs, as we speak, preparing to lay down her life if it means saving yours."

His words humbled me. "I never wanted that. Not from any

of you."

"Well you have it, Flor. Don't waste what we're offering you by putting yourself in any more danger than you need to." His hands dropped from my face.

I stepped forward and wrapped my arms around the stranger in front of me. Although in the dim light of the basement, it was much easier to pretend that the arms which returned my embrace in a crushing bear hug, actually belonged to my best friend.

"I love you, Flor," he murmured against my hair.

Fighting back the tears, I kept my face buried against his chest as I asked, "Always?"

I could hear the smile in his voice as he replied. "And forever."

The sound of excited voices above us caught my attention, and then Freya's voice floated down the basement stairs to us. "Flora, Finlay, they're back."

My heart quickened with relief at Lyall's safe return. Finlay released me without hesitation, and he gave me a reassuring nod as I fired him a last glance through the gloom before bounding up the stairs to check that Lyall and Artair were unharmed.

When I burst back into the lighted room above and saw Lyall unhurt, I bounded across the room and hugged him tightly.

He smiled and kissed my forehead. "See, I told you we'd be fine, love."

"How did it go?" Finlay asked as he appeared in the doorway. "Did you see what you wanted to see?"

Lyall and Artair frowned at each other, and Lyall quickly released me so he could sit down at the table. We all followed his lead and took our own seats as a hush settled over the room.

"Truthfully, it's worse than we had thought," Artair admitted.

Enid bit her lip. "How much worse?"

"He has around two hundred Supers." Lyall's words brought silence and looks of horror to the faces of everyone around the table.

"They're going to take us apart," I finally managed to whisper.

"Two hundred Supers?" Finlay shook his head in disbelief.

"It's not as awful as it sounds," Artair insisted. "We have an equal amount of Draugur."

"We do have the animal souls," Enid suggested helpfully.

When Artair and Lyall stared blankly at her, Enid quickly filled them in on our latest recruits.

"So, it's not as bad as it sounds." Lyall eased himself back into his chair but his usual overconfident poise didn't come so easily today.

"The question is, did you manage to get the spell set up in the basement?" Artair looked affectionately at Enid as he spoke.

She nodded. "I did. It's complete magical lockdown in there."

Artair reached out to lay his hand gently over hers. "Well done."

Lyall spoke with the calm confidence of a seasoned battle

commander, and I wondered, not for the first time, how he managed it so easily. "So, our plan still remains the same. Flora will deploy her loyal Draugur to fight the Supers. If we can get them back here, they can be thrown in to the basement until we're ready to deal with them."

"The animal souls will happily help with that," Enid suggested.

Lyall frowned. "I think half of the animal souls should help with the Supers and half should stay close to Flora to protect her while she works on Sluag's soul."

Artair nodded. "Agreed."

"What will the rest of you be doing?" I dreaded the answer to my question.

"We'll be fighting amongst the Draugur and animal souls. We need to lead them and keep them right," Bear replied.

Finlay looked to Lyall. "Lyall, you need to be close enough for Flora to draw on your energy. You could do with staying behind the protection of the animal souls."

Lyall shook his head. "I'm not hiding behind anyone. I can stay close enough to Flora to share my energy with her and still play a part in the fighting."

I shuddered as I thought back to my dream. "You have to stay away from Sluag. Promise me?"

Lyall levelled his gaze at me. "That's not going to come true, love. It was just a dream."

"Even so, I don't think we need to take unnecessary risks," I insisted.

"Flora's right, Lyall. We should do anything we can to stop her dream from coming true," Freya said firmly.

Grudgingly, Lyall nodded. "All right, I'll stay close to Flora. I'd prefer it that way anyhow."

Bear planted his sun-tanned arms on the tabletop. "So, I guess the only question left, is, when do we attack?"

I bit my lip. I felt as though we were still so unprepared. Although I suspected I would feel the same even if we had a hundred years to make our plans.

"The sooner the better," Artair offered.

Lyall nodded. "I agree, the quicker we attack, the less Supers Sluag can create."

Finlay spoke up. "There's something I think we should do first."

"What is it?" I asked him.

"Just because we can't bury Pen, doesn't mean that she can't have a memorial service. I think we need to lay her to rest before we go to war."

He didn't say any more, but I knew he was thinking that most of us wouldn't be coming back from the fight, so we should say goodbye while we still had the chance.

"Finlay's right," Freya agreed.

Lyall stood up and looked at me as he spoke. "I know a place that's perfect."

I got to my feet and nodded in agreement. "Let's go."

CHAPTER
29

The journey out to the stand of willows which Lyall had chosen to be Pen's final resting place, was quiet—giving each of us too much time to think about the upcoming battle.

As we made our way through the dense forest, the sunlight shone through the canopy above and dappled the floor beneath our feet with spots of gold. It was peaceful and beautiful, but I suspected that none of us were really enjoying the serenity of our surroundings.

I stole glances at the faces of my Dion as they walked alongside me. They all looked tired, pale, and haunted—I knew I looked the same.

No one spoke, and I was sure it was because we were all caught up in our own imaginations. Each of us was weaving an individual nightmare inside our heads of how the war was going to end.

My personal nightmare was a perfect replay of my dream. Over and over inside my mind, Lyall would die and Finlay would disappear forever, while each of my other Dion was struck down by a different Super.

I was drawn out of my daydream by the feel of warm fingertips brushing against my own cold hands. As Lyall slipped his fingers through mine, I smiled at him, grateful for the distraction.

He returned my smile. "How are you doing, love?"

I gripped his hand tightly. "Okay. I'll be better when this is over with and we're all still alive."

He looked so broken in that moment I felt as though someone had knocked the breath out of me. His amber eyes lost their fire, and I would have sworn his lower lip almost quivered as he fought to offer me a rueful smile.

"Yeah me too, love." His voice sounded cracked.

"Is this it?" Enid called back softly as she approached a stand of ancient willows whose trunks rose toward the sky before their branches cascaded back down toward the ground. I noticed the branches of the trees closest to the water trailed gently over the surface of the loch, making tiny ripples as they swayed in the breeze. Each tree had its own perfect image reflected back at it on the mirror of calm, green water.

"This is it," Lyall confirmed.

I gave his hand a final squeeze before letting go. "This is perfect. Thank you," I murmured.

As we entered the grove, the bright green leaves rustled softly in the breeze. That, mixed with the sound of the water of Loch Ness lapping gently against the shore, cast a blanket of calm over me.

We had each brought freshly picked flowers to lay at the grove. Now all of us placed our flowers on the ground as we stood in a circle beneath the green canopy. We hadn't planned anything that would happen, past getting here, and I looked around the circle, wondering who would speak first.

Finlay took a step forward so he was inside the circle. His eyes were moist, and his head was bowed, but he spoke up vibrantly as he talked of the woman whom he had called mother.

"Penthesilea was an incredible woman. She was strong and brave, but she was also kind and wise. She took each and every one of us under her wing when we had no one else left in the world.

"Although Pen lost her first Soul Keeper, it was through no fault of her own. She loved Aiden and would have given her life ten times over to see him safe. The reason she lost the man she loved, was because of Sluag, and that is why we will do whatever it takes to finish him, forever. In honour of Penthesilea Michaelson."

We bowed our heads and murmured our agreement.

Freya spoke next. "I knew Pen longer than all of you. I didn't always want to be a Dion, most of you know that. I've been pretty unbearable sometimes, in fact. But, Pen was the one person on whom I could rely, and she made me into the Dion that I am today. No matter what happens, I will do her proud."

When it came to Lyall's speech, my cheeks were already wet. I had heard so many stories about the different ways that

Pen had touched our lives.

"I know most of you don't know my whole story. But, you do know that I killed someone, someone innocent." Lyall clenched his fists so tightly as he spoke, that his knuckles turned milk-white.

"I had lost everything when Pen found me, and if she hadn't brought me to Castle Dion and fixed all of the things that were wrong with me, then I probably would have lost my own life too."

I felt sadness well up inside me as he spoke. I knew the full story of Lyall's childhood, and it wasn't a happy one.

"So, there are two ways that I can pay Penthesilea back for all of the things she did. Firstly, I'm going to make sure that I protect our Soul Keeper at all costs. Nothing is happening to Flora, as long as I'm here to stop it. Secondly, once we put Sluag down, we're taking back Castle Dion. It doesn't belong to the devil. It belongs to us and so help me, we will be sleeping in our own beds again before this day is done."

As the other Dion cheered aloud, I realised Lyall hadn't just intended a memorial speech. That had been a battle-cry. It was his call to arms and his way of letting the other Dion know we weren't backing down without the mother of all fights.

In that moment, I understood what Pen had meant all of those months ago when she told me how important it was to choose the right Dion to bond with. Lyall was the leader I had needed by my side, the protector who would keep me safe from harm, and he was the one person whom I could trust to keep my heart safe.

I took a step toward my bonded Dion, wanting to thank him for his strength. But, I was stopped in my tracks by the sound of a solitary pair of hands clapping slowly and mockingly.

We all fell into a shocked silence as Sluag walked slowly across the clearing until he reached the centre, still clapping his bony hands as he went. I glanced around our circle, and my stomach tightened in fear as I took in the figures of perhaps thirty Super Draugur standing behind us to form their own circle. We were trapped and outnumbered.

"Ahh, what a rousing speech, young Lyall. Again, I lament your refusal to join the winning side." Sluag stopped clapping and instead stroked his scaly chin thoughtfully. "Unless, of course, you have changed your mind, perhaps?"

"I've told you this before. I'd rather die a thousand times over than even consider joining you, monster." Lyall curled his lip in disgust.

Sluag shrugged. "A shame. But, your death is going to be arranged much quicker than you anticipate, I suspect, Dion."

I studied Sluag intently before speaking. "It's okay, he's not really here. He's just projecting like he did in the cottage." I frowned at the Supers. "I don't think I can say the same for them, though."

Sluag threw back his head and roared with laughter. His mirth continued for so long I was just starting to think he had gone completely mad. Then his mouth snapped shut and, his head twisted to look at me.

"Just projecting, Flora?" His voice was mocking. "Are you

so sure of that?"

Before I had a chance to answer, he darted across the clearing with unnatural speed until he had his bony fingers wrapped around Bear's throat. Sluag pushed him backward until he thudded to a stop against a willow trunk.

The brawny Dion paled instantly as Sluag's monstrous grip on his throat cut off not just his air supply but the blood supply to his head too.

Freya howled and dived at Sluag but he simply swatted her away as though she were made of feathers.

"Still think I'm not really here, Little Dreamer?"

"Sluag, stop?" I called as I rushed forward.

My attack was swiftly ended as two firm hands wrapped around my waist and yanked me back.

"Sorry, love, can't let you do that. We need you alive."

"Lyall, let me go," I hissed.

Sluag bellowed in delight. "Ahh, a lovers' tiff." His fingers tightened around Bear's throat, and Bear's eyes bulged from their sockets.

"Please?" I murmured as Freya launched herself at Sluag again, only to be batted aside once more.

Then, just as quickly as he had grabbed Bear, Sluag abruptly let go and the Dion slid down the tree to land on the grassy floor in a broken heap. Sluag crossed the clearing again until he was facing me. Lyall pushed his body in front of mine defensively.

"Loyal Lyall." Sluag shook his head. "I can't decide whether to kill you in front of Flora, or if I should kill her in front of you."

"Try it," Lyall growled.

Sluag was silent for a moment before he took a single, menacing step toward us.

"Oh, I will. Not now, however. This is my first experience of complete liberation from the Endwood. My priority is to go and take my place inside my new castle. Flora knows I have a hankering for a throne."

My heart sank as I realised he was talking about Castle Dion.

"It's not yours," I snarled.

Sluag turned his back on us both, his cloak billowing out behind him as he stalked imperiously across the grove, followed closely by his Supers.

"Then come and take it from me, Little Dreamer. I believe you've seen how the battle of Castle Dion ends. How brave are you feeling?"

I closed my eyes, but I could still hear his laughter long after he had completely disappeared amongst the dense surrounding woodland.

CHAPTER 30

Once we were certain Sluag and his Draugur had completely gone, Lyall stepped aside and finally allowed me to run toward where Freya leaned over an unmoving Bear.

"You have to be okay," she was whispering, over and over again.

I dropped to my knees beside her and pressed my fingers against the pulse point in his neck. Part of my tour guide training had included first aid, in the event a visitor keeled over on site, and I knew the basics pretty well.

I quickly found a pulse and also confirmed he was breathing by himself. Lyall handed me his jacket, and I laid it over Bear to keep him warm.

"Freya, he's okay. He's going to be okay." I wrapped my arm around her shoulders as I spoke.

She turned wide blue eyes on me—they didn't look as ice cold as they had when I had first met her.

"Do you swear it, Flora?" she rasped.

I nodded. "I swear."

Bowing her head until her forehead came to rest on Bear's chest, Freya breathed out deeply. "Thank you."

As Bear began to wake, my lips curved up in the hint of a smile. "Don't ever try and tell me that he means nothing to you again, though."

She looked from Bear's confused face to mine, and her face broke into a grin. "Tell anyone and you're dead to me, Soul Keeper."

I looked around at the group of Dion who surrounded us at a little distance. "Might be a little late for that I think."

But Bear was awake now, and Freya's attention was all for him.

"So much for the element of surprise," Artair said as I rejoined the others.

"I hadn't expected the veil to fall so quickly," Lyall admitted.

"We need to go back to the terminal and regroup. Attacking Castle Dion isn't going to be as easy as attacking the Endwood." Finlay ran his hands through his hair in the way he always did when he was worried. It was strange to watch the gesture performed by his new body.

"Agreed," Lyall said.

"If we're heading back now, we might need to give Bear a little help," Enid suggested.

"Bear doesn't need any help." Bear's voice was slightly pained but still full of his usual wicked humour as he stood up.

191

We all smiled in relief to see him on his feet so quickly, until he stumbled slightly and lost his balance. If Freya hadn't been waiting to catch him, he would probably have ended up on his ass.

"Bear is going to have to shut up and accept some help," Freya growled as she supported his weight.

He grinned at her. "A get-well kiss would probably fix me in no time, hotness."

"Unless you want to end up on your ass again, I suggest you shut up and start walking." Although her words were harsh, Freya's face was lit by a smile as she spoke.

That was obviously good enough for Bear, and he beamed at her as she helped him to start walking.

As I watched them, a sudden thought hit me, and I stopped dead in my tracks.

"What is it, love?" Lyall asked in a worried voice.

My voice was stricken. "The Everwood. If the veil has fallen, then the rogues will have passed through it. I have to go and check on my pure souls, Lyall."

"I'll come with you," he said firmly.

I shook my head. "No, get them safely back to the terminal. There won't be a single rogue left in the Everwood by now. They'll be desperately trying to steal themselves a body in the mortal world."

"Are you sure?"

"I'll be fine. Look after the other Dion."

He finally agreed. "All right, love, but if you're not with us in two hours, I'm coming for you."

I didn't hesitate. I faded from where I stood in the mortal world and reappeared in the Everwood an instant later.

I hadn't been ready for the devastation that I found.

The first thing I noticed was the colour of the sky. It was as though blood had been spilled across the roof of the world. This wasn't the red-gold dawn that had promised itself in the Endwood. This was a dark and brooding sunset, the end of the day, the end of an era. The Everwood was breaking apart before my eyes.

A cold wind whipped through the trees, tearing the blue flowers from their branches and scattering the petals across the grass. Grass which was no longer completely lush and green but a straw-yellow colour instead.

I looked around me, desperately calling out to my pure souls. One or two appeared and hesitantly drifted toward me.

"What happened here?" I whispered to them.

A tiny blue orb trembled as it answered me.

The rogues came, Flora. There were thousands of them. They attacked the pure souls, and then they left for the mortal world.

I felt a blaze of fury inside me. "Did they hurt any of you?"

They did try, but we were safe because of the Everwood. It protected us somehow.

I was wracked with guilt. "I should have been here to keep you safe. I failed you."

The little blue light was joined by another soul, and they

gently grazed against my cheeks.

No, Flora. You shouldn't be here right now. You must fight the Host of the Unforgiven Dead, or all is lost.

I thought back to my conversation with Sluag. He wouldn't use that name any longer. He now considered himself "Lord of Everything".

I turned back to the tiny orbs and was relieved to see they had been joined by others now.

"What will happen here, if we lose?" I asked quietly.

The tiny blue orb bobbed up and down as though in despair before it replied inside my mind.

Then the sun will set, and there will be nowhere for pure souls to go.

I looked around me at the wasteland that was my Everwood. The trees were dying, the grass was damaged, and the sky burned with an anger that seemed to foretell the end of the world.

"I can't let this happen," I murmured, more to myself than anyone else. I couldn't let this world fall apart.

"I won't fail you," I promised aloud to the gathering crowd of pure souls.

Just as I began to imagine myself back in the mortal world, the little blue orb called out inside my mind.

Flora?

I paused and gave my attention to the pure soul. "What did you want?"

You must remember that "A Blood Inheritance Secures

Allegiance."

I nodded at the soul. "I do remember. It already helped us, a lot."

The little orb burned brightly as though in frustration.

No, Flora. You don't understand.

The tiny light bobbed up to my ear as though it were trying to tell me something that was completely confidential. When it did start to speak inside my head, it even sounded as though it were whispering.

My eyes widened in surprise as the soul relayed its information to me. Once it had finished telling me everything it needed me to know, the tiny orb looped through the air until it hovered in front of my face once more.

"Are you sure?" I asked in disbelief.

Quite sure. The reply was firm inside my mind.

A slow smile spread across my face, and just like that, hope was renewed. "Will it work?"

The tiny orb bobbed once, and I knew it had shrugged its metaphorical shoulders.

"Let's hope so." I reached out and gently touched my fingers against the little orb.

A final question came unbidden to my lips. Just two words. "And Lyall?"

The little blue light trembled before me as I held my breath and waited for its reply.

I'm sorry, Soul Keeper.

I felt as though I was dying inside. "I understand. Thank

you," I whispered as I faded from the Everwood.

Good luck, Flora Bast. We will be waiting for your return.

CHAPTER 31

I was relieved to see Bear back to his usual self when I arrived at the terminal. He was perched on the edge of the table and stuffing a sandwich into his mouth while he talked about how he had stood up to Sluag.

"Sat down for Sluag, more like," Lyall grumbled to himself as I crept up behind him and wrapped my arms around his waist.

Lyall almost hit the roof until he realised it was me, and then he admonished me. "Flora, don't sneak up on me like that. I could have hurt you."

"Sorry, I'm just happy to see you and to see our casualty is feeling better too." I nodded in Bear's direction.

Lyall rolled his eyes. "Oh, he's feeling better all right. Can't get him to shut up."

I smiled. "I think Freya is very happy to see Bear's okay."

He narrowed his eyes at me. "What happened in the Everwood?"

I looked down at my feet, trying to fight back tears.

Although the tiny pure soul had given me some hope, it had stolen more from me when it confirmed what I already knew. I couldn't save Lyall.

Lyall caught my chin with his hand and tilted my face up to look at him. "Is everything okay, love?"

I fired a glance at the door. "Take a walk with me?"

He nodded. "Of course, I will."

We walked through the trees in comfortable silence, until we reached the shady banks of the loch. This part of the shoreline was covered by a thick tangle of trees, which made me feel as though Lyall and I were the only two people left in the world.

Lyall sat down next to the water and patted the ground next to him, indicating I should do the same.

When I sat down next to him and tucked my legs underneath me, he spoke. "What happened, love? Is it as bad as you thought?"

I sighed. "In some ways yes, and in some ways no."

I went on to explain the crazy sunset and the damage to the trees and grass. I told Lyall all about my conversation with the souls, but when I got to the final part about the blood inheritance securing allegiance, I skipped past and finished the story.

I wasn't sure why I chose not to tell Lyall about the things the soul had told me. I was pretty sure it was probably because I didn't want him to have false hope for our victory, and I was also certain he would try even harder to get Sluag out of his body if he knew the truth.

"We need to strike at Castle Dion sooner rather than later, Lyall. I can't leave those souls like that." My voice trembled.

Lyall stared out over the loch, watching a thick mist that was rolling slowly across the water.

"I know, love. I'm just worried that if we rush into this, we'll get ourselves killed."

"Lyall, people all over the world are going to die now the rogues are free to poach their bodies. We have to move quickly," I retorted.

"Agreed." He carried on watching the mist as he spoke. It was as though he wasn't really listening to me.

"Lyall," I snapped, and he turned his head to study my face.

"We have to stop him before any more people die, Lyall. Why are you so distant?"

"I'm sorry, love. I guess I'm just holding back because I know that once we march on the castle, that's it—there's no turning back."

I frowned at him, confused. "I know you well enough to know that you aren't afraid of Sluag."

He smiled bitterly. "No, I'm not afraid of Sluag. I'm not afraid to die either, love."

I felt a ball of ice form inside my stomach when he talked about dying.

He carried on speaking as though he hadn't noticed my discomfort. "You, Flora."

"What about me?" I asked.

"You're what I'm afraid of. When Sluag talked about killing

you in front of me, he knew exactly what that would do to me. You're my biggest weakness, love. I can't watch you die, and I can't live without you. That's the truth of why I don't want to start this thing." He rested his elbows on his knees and dropped his head into his hands as he spoke.

Taking a deep breath, I reached out and laid my hand gingerly on top of his head. My fingers absently twisted through his dark hair, stroking him gently as I did when he was in wolf form.

"Lyall, I'm terrified I'm going to lose you. I can't even let myself think about how that looks. That's why you have to stay away from Sluag. If my dream was right, then he's the one who's going to kill you."

He laughed softly. "I don't think your dream was a premonition, Flora. You're no seer. You're a Soul Keeper."

"But, the prophecies in the manuscripts still say you will die," I argued.

"And I'm okay with that. If it means that I get to save the girl and the rest of the world." He winked at me.

Anger and fear welled up inside me. "No, Lyall. You don't get to just blow into my life, turn everything upside down, and make me fall in love with you, before riding off into the sunset on your bloody white horse to die."

I tried to stand, but he caught my wrist and pulled me against his chest. I fought against him, punching, kicking, and crying. "No, I won't let you do it. I won't, I won't."

He held on tightly until I inevitably wore myself out and

collapsed against him, breathing hard.

"Shh, love, shh." He stroked my hair as he soothed me.

Eventually I couldn't cry any more. The sobs quieted down to whimpers and then became huge gulping breaths as I tried to get air into my oxygen-starved body.

His voice was soft and quiet. "I hate myself for leaving you, you know. I'm so sorry, if it does happen, love. It was never my intention to hurt you and deep down inside, I think you know it."

I sat back from him, and this time he let me go. I wiped furiously at my tear-stained cheeks. "I know you didn't mean to hurt me," I whispered.

He leaned forward and brushed his fingers beneath my eyes, capturing the remains of my tears.

"I love you, Flora Bast. I lost myself to you the moment I met you, and I always knew that I would die for you if that was what it took to keep you safe."

He opened his arms to me, and I let him envelop me as I lay between his legs with my back against his chest. We sat in silence and watched until the glassy sheen of the loch disappeared completely beneath the encroaching mist.

After what felt like a lifetime, he shifted behind me. "Are you still awake, love?"

I nodded. "It's time to go, isn't it?"

I felt him return my nod behind me.

As we stood up, he took both of my hands in his. "I swear, Flora, if I can stay with you, I will. I'm in no hurry to die, love. If there's any way that means we can both walk out of this together, then I'm gonna snatch it with both hands."

I stared back in to his amber wolf eyes. "I swear, if there's any way I can stop myself from losing you, then I'm going to take it."

He leaned down slowly and laid the gentlest kiss against my forehead in the usual spot. "As long as it's not at the expense of humanity, then count me in, love."

CHAPTER
32

When we arrived back at the terminal, the others were preparing everything they would need for the march on Castle Dion. The loyal Draugur were milling around outside the outbuilding they had called home for the last few weeks.

Lyall snapped straight back into war commander mode as soon as we returned to the company of the other Dion. It took a few deep breaths for me to ground myself as I watched him work, realising I might never see the Lyall I had just spent the last couple of hours with, again.

My eyes scanned the Draugur and Dion alike, until they finally settled on Finlay. He clearly sensed I was watching him and turned to smile grimly at me.

I beckoned him to come to me, and he nodded before turning back to quickly finish packing a bag with spare clothes—obviously replacements for what we were wearing, if we had to shift during the fight.

When he finished up and came trotting over to me, I

grabbed his hand and pulled him quickly out of the clearing that surrounded the terminal, so we were standing behind the cover of the tall trees that surrounded us.

"Whoa, Flor. What's up?" He looked back toward the others as he spoke.

Although I knew with absolute certainty Finlay had to know the truth of what the little blue soul had told me in the Everwood, I bit my lip with worry as I hesitated in asking him to give up even more.

What if he refuses to help me?

"Flora. Are you okay?" His eyes were filled with concern.

I nodded, before taking a deep breath and plunging into my story. I told Finlay everything, with the exception of one tiny piece of information that even now, I wasn't sure could be true.

Finlay's eyes grew wider as I related what the tiny, blue soul had told me. As I neared the end of the story, he started to understand what I was asking of him, and I studied his face intently as I spoke, certain I saw fear drift across his features for an instant.

When I stopped talking, I stood as still as a statue and waited to hear what he would say.

"Did you tell Lyall?"

I shook my head. "No."

"Why not, Flor?"

"Because he'll insist on giving me every last drop of energy he has, to make sure we succeed in pushing Sluag out of his body. That *will* kill him, Finlay."

"He's going to do that anyway, Flor."

I closed my eyes, knowing that Finlay was right.

Finlay shifted uncomfortably from foot to foot. "What happens if you *need* to take all of Lyall's energy to force Sluag's soul out?"

I opened my eyes again. "Then I won't..." My voice trailed off into a soundless whisper, and I bowed my head in shame.

He frowned at me. "I'll do everything I can, Flor."

I looked up at him. "Really?"

He nodded. "Yes, but you have to promise me that you won't let Sluag ruin the world by trying to save Lyall's life. He wouldn't want that, Flor. You know he wouldn't. That's exactly why you didn't tell him, isn't it?"

"I know what I need to do, Finlay. I just never expected to have to sacrifice the man I love to save the world." I fought back tears, determined I wouldn't cry again.

Finlay shook his head in disbelief. "If you hadn't been so determined to keep my memories and give me a new body all those months ago, then I wouldn't be here now. How did you know I was supposed to be there for the end, Flor?"

I shook my head. "I didn't, Finlay. I fought to keep your memories and your soul here because I couldn't stand to think of a world without my best friend in it."

He smiled at me. "Well, knowing what we know now, it seems like a bloody good job you did, huh?"

I bit my lip. "I think fate might have had more than a little bit of a hand in this."

"If fate is on our side, then that must mean we're meant to win this war," he suggested hopefully.

I started back toward the terminal. "I hope so, Finlay. I really do."

"Flora?" He called after me.

I turned back to look at him questioningly.

His eyes darkened. "Lyall's one of my best friends. Truthfully, I don't know if I will be able to stand aside and let him die—even to save the world."

I gave him a relieved smile. *He understood me.*

His next words were much less comforting. "But I do know that if you try and sacrifice yourself for him, I will stop you. I love you too much to watch you die, Flor. So, don't even think about it."

Pausing momentarily, I gave Finlay a stiff nod and started back toward the terminal. I felt hollow inside.

Freya spoke to me as I approached the pile of supplies that waited just outside the terminal door. "I think we're almost ready to leave, Flora."

Pushing Finlay's last words to me out of my mind, I smiled at Freya. "Let's hope we have everything we need."

She tipped her head in Lyall's direction and grumbled. "If you listen to Captain Harris over there, you'd think we were a bunch of novices who don't have a clue."

I looked at Lyall and smiled appreciatively. "He's pretty damn good at this isn't he?"

Freya harrumphed. "Pretty damn good at being a pain in

the ass."

Before I walked away, I laid a gentle hand on Freya's arm. "Don't let this thing start without telling him exactly how you feel."

She scrunched up her perfect nose and stopped what she was doing. "You want me to tell Lyall he's a pain in the ass?"

I snorted and pointed my chin in the opposite direction. Her eyes followed my lead and landed on Bear.

"Tell him," I murmured.

We both watched the cocky, Irish Dion juggling three knives, before dropping them into a waiting backpack.

Freya brought her eyes back to mine. "I will," was all she said.

I nodded in satisfaction and made my way to the door of the terminal. I wanted to get the photograph of my parents. If I was going to die today, then I wanted my family with me when it happened.

I crossed the main floor of the terminal. Although it was dawn, the dense tangle of trees outside, coupled with the tiny windows of the building didn't let much light through. The room was gloomy and dust kicked up from my feet as I walked into the room I shared with Lyall.

Even though it was dark in here, the room had become familiar to me now. I quickly found the drawer of a battered, wooden desk that was pushed in to the corner of the room. My hand closed around the picture of my family, and I lifted it up to my face to place a kiss on the shiny paper before tucking it safely into the pocket of my jeans.

As my eyes adjusted to the gloom, I suddenly noticed a small blue box on the end of the bed that hadn't been there when I was last in this room.

I walked over to the bed, and my hand closed around the velvet, ring-box. My heart raced as I opened it up, and a sheet of folded paper fell out and landed on the floor. I bent down to retrieve the paper and then flicked on the dim lamp at the side of the bed.

In the brighter light, I noticed a glint of metal inside the box. When I peered inside, I saw a silver ring that had been wrought into the most beautiful and intricate shape I had ever seen.

The ring itself was made out of several thin strands that had been cast to create an effect that was strikingly similar to the branches of the Síorraidh trees. At intervals along the branches, there were minute flowers that were a complete replica of the blue blooms that were currently scattered through the Everwood by the cold winds.

It was beautiful.

I slipped the ring on to my finger before unfolding the piece of paper and reading the words that were written upon it.

Flora,

I reckon you and I are going to spend a lot of time arguing over the next few hours, love, and that's not how I wanted to spend the rest of our time together.

I had this made by Eric at the library. He's a surprisingly good silversmith. I was going to give it to you myself, but somehow time just seems to have run out.

I think Eric told you that the trees in the Everwood are called Síorraidh trees, but I don't think he told you what the name actually means.

It means eternal, Flora.

I couldn't really think of a better way to tell you how I feel about you, or to let you know that no matter what happens, I'll always be with you, love.

My Soul Eternal,

Lyall

CHAPTER 33

As soon as I stepped out of the terminal and into the dawn light, my eyes picked out his amber wolf orbs from across the clearing. He cocked a brow at me inquisitively, and I raised my hand with the palm toward me so he could see the silver band around my finger.

His huge smile was equal parts beautiful and soul-destroying.

I was just about to cross the clearing and go to him, when Artair spoke up. "Okay. That's it. We're ready to move out."

We each collected our equipment and supplies from the pile in the centre of the clearing. Freya was handing out weapons to the loyal Draugur and giving them instructions to meet us on the other side of the loch.

We intended to take two boats across the water. There was no way we had enough room for the Draugur to join us, but they were able to get to our meeting point—around two miles south of Castle Dion—much quicker than we could on foot.

I dropped my hands to the belt around my waist, double-checking that the Síorraidh box was safe and secure. I breathed a sigh of relief when my hands found the delicately carved surface that mimicked the ring on my hand.

I wondered, not for the first time, if the box really would hold Sluag's soul for eternity. It seemed so ordinary and much too fragile to be able to cage the soul of a monster that was thousands of years old.

Still, it was all we had. It had to be enough, or the mortal world would be overrun with evil before the week was out.

We reached the moored-up boats that bobbed expectantly on the calm waters. Lyall, Artair, and I would take one boat and Finlay, Bear, and Freya would take the other. Enid wouldn't be joining us as she would lead the animal souls to Castle Dion separately.

Everyone took a seat in their respective vessel except Artair. He stood on the grassy shore and embraced Enid.

"Keep in touch and don't take any risks." Artair spoke roughly, and I knew he was thinking back to the day Mara was killed.

Enid smiled at him. "Stop worrying. I'm not the terrified little idiot who arrived here all those months ago with Flora and Lyall, Art."

Only Enid called Artair, Art.

He leaned down and gave her a quick kiss. "I know, you're bloody amazing. But, be safe, okay?"

She turned to make her way back up the bank to wave us

off before heading to the Everwood. I had warned her that it wasn't a pretty sight, and I hoped she was ready to face the desolation she would find in my kingdom. I also hoped all of her animal souls were safe and sound.

Artair jumped into our boat, and it rocked unsteadily as he untied the rope that tethered us to the land and pushed us off across the green expanse of water. I swallowed down a lump in my throat as I realised that no matter what happened now, we weren't ever coming back to the terminal.

It wasn't that I would miss the derelict building. The complete opposite, in fact. But, as I looked around at the faces of my Dion, I wondered for the thousandth time how many of us were going to survive until the end of today.

My eyes landed on Finlay, and I sent up a silent prayer, to no one in particular that he would keep up his end of the deal. He was the only chance we had at winning this war, and how quickly he managed to help me bring Sluag to heel could be vital in whether or not Lyall walked away from the fight.

Lyall sat opposite me in the tiny boat. He rowed slowly and I found myself almost hypnotised by the rhythm of the oars as they dipped into the water before rising in the air to scatter sparkling droplets through the misty morning air.

"Thank you," I whispered to him.

"For what?" he teased.

I thought about my answer for a moment before finally settling on a response.

"For eternity."

He nodded at that and continued to row sedately.

Artair's voice grabbed our attention. "I think we've made the right decision to bring the boats in at a distance from Castle Dion. It should give us a chance to approach unnoticed and hopefully try and work out exactly what we're up against."

Lyall frowned. "Even if we do manage to spy on the castle, Sluag is expecting us. He knows we'll be looking for weaknesses, and he'll make sure to lay as many traps and lies as possible."

"Not a positive perspective, Lyall," Artair growled.

"An honest one, though, mate. He's gained the leverage he wanted by breaking out of the Endwood so soon. He wanted to force our hand, and he's going to make us pay for every rushed decision and every mistake."

Artair studied the thick wall of fog as though he might somehow be able to see through it and pick out the western shore of the loch.

"Let's hope not. Sluag's idea of making us pay usually involves a lot of blood."

"I'm not letting him spill another drop of our blood." The fury in my voice made both of them turn to look at me.

"It's a war, Flora. Blood will be spilled. It's inevitable." Artair spoke softly.

I bit my lip and nodded. Artair was right. I could no more promise there would be no more bloodshed than I could promise I would reach out and touch the moon.

"It's all about that box, love." I looked down as Lyall stopped rowing for a moment to reach out and gently nudge the

213

Síorraidh box that hung at my waist.

"The sooner we can get Sluag out of his body, the sooner the bloodshed stops," he finished.

"The only thing we really need to worry about, is whether or not Flora's Draugur can hold on to the Supers long enough to get them into the spelled cells," Artair said.

I hated how dependent on the Draugur we were. I thought again of how grateful I was that we had the animal souls as extra back-up.

"There we are," Artair murmured. I lifted my head up to follow his gaze, and my eyes managed to pick out the faint outline of land through the mist.

A low whistle brought all of our attention to the other boat. Finlay pointed to the upcoming land and then mouthed the word, *Supers*.

As we turned back to look, I managed to pick out the shadowy figures of two Supers who stalked slowly back and forth along the shore. They were guarding the exact spot that we had hoped to moor the boats up on.

"Guards. Dammit, he knew we'd come by boat," Lyall hissed under his breath as he stopped rowing.

"We'll have to get out elsewhere," I suggested.

"He'll have guards posted all the way along the shore, Flora." Artair tapped his fingers distractedly against the side of the boat.

"We can't kill them, and we don't have any Draugur with us to send against them. What can we do?" I asked in despair.

The other boat drifted up against ours with a gentle clunk.

"Any ideas?" Finlay asked.

"Other than waiting for Flora's Draugur to show up? Nope, not really," Lyall replied angrily.

As we sat and pondered our predicament, I noticed a sudden movement in the bushes behind the Super that was nearest to us. As the Draugur burst out of the foliage and attacked the guard, we started to move forward as Lyall began furiously rowing again.

The two Supers were easily subdued by the torrent of Draugur that started to stream out of hiding, and I breathed a sigh of relief.

"This is a disaster," Bear shouted.

I looked at him, confused.

"They're not exactly stealthy, Flora. If any other guards along the shore hear what's going on, they'll be off to let Sluag know we're here before you can say 'hello, would you like to sacrifice me?'"

Artair growled, "Shit, Lyall, he's right. We need to get this finished and quickly."

Lyall's arms and shoulders flexed as he put every ounce of effort he had into getting us to the shore before our cover was broken.

As soon as the boats bumped against the grass, my Dion were over the side and running for the struggling Draugur. The Supers were shrieking at the top of their lungs, and I knew it was only to try to alert the other sentries.

Lyall and Artair both reached the Supers, and without hesitation, they each grabbed one of the monsters' heads and twisted until their necks snapped with a bone-jarring crunch.

The Supers temporarily disabled bodies slumped to the ground, and I breathed out in relief.

Lyall turned to the group of loyal Draugur who were milling around sheepishly.

"That's what you do to keep them quiet, okay? Now tie them up, attach some stones to their arms and legs, and then drop them in to the loch. It won't kill them, but it'll hopefully keep them quiet long enough for us to go undiscovered."

If we haven't been discovered already, I thought to myself.

CHAPTER 34

Once the Supers had been disposed of and the boats were hauled out of the water and hidden in the thick bushes that grew next to the shore, we were ready to march on the castle.

Artair suggested we strike out inland for a mile before turning north and heading toward Castle Dion. Lyall and Finlay agreed.

"It makes sense. Sluag will expect us to follow the waterline to the castle. He probably won't have invested as many sentries into watching the woodland," Finlay said approvingly.

It was slow going through the tangled foliage and we were continually under threat of discovery from random Draugur but after around two hours of walking we finally spotted the towers of Castle Dion.

I wasn't ready for the pang of homesickness that overwhelmed me as the dilapidated ramparts came into view.

"It feels so strange to look at it from this perspective," Freya whispered.

"We aren't getting close enough to see it in restored condition, at least not yet," Lyall confirmed as he stared at the ruins.

"I think it feels right that it looks like this when Sluag has control of it," I said, and they all nodded in agreement.

We had brought food and water with us and decided that now would be a good time to rest up and wait for Enid to arrive with her animal souls.

Artair had been relieved to speak with Enid on the phone when we had stopped to rest. She had reassured him all was well, and they were only a few hours away from our location. She had to lead her animal souls around the loch at the south side so it had taken them a while to catch us up.

"Once Enid gets here with the animal souls, our group will be too large to go unnoticed for long. We need to try and find out as much as we possibly can before she arrives," Artair suggested.

"What better way to spy on a castle, than from the air?" Freya grinned.

Finlay nodded at them both. "You're right, you two need to shift and provide us with a birds-eye view."

Before Freya changed into her raven alter, Bear grabbed her around the waist and pulled her against him. Freya pressed her hands against his chest, blushing furiously.

"Bear, what are you doing? Let me go," she hissed.

"Not until you promise to be careful, hotness." He laughed, unfazed by her tantrum.

"Let me—oh, fine, fine. I promise I'll be careful, okay?"

Freya stopped struggling, and when Bear leaned down to place a gentle kiss against her lips, she leaned into him and kissed him back.

I smiled and dropped my eyes to give them some privacy. Only when I heard the shriek of a raven calling did I look up to see Freya joining Artair in the air, before they both winged their way in the direction of Castle Dion.

Be safe, both of you. I called out in my mind.

As they disappeared above the treetops, I felt a hand brush against my own. Turning, I allowed Lyall to lift my hand to his lips and place a gentle kiss against my Síorraidh ring.

"Thank you for wearing it, love," he murmured.

I gasped in surprise as I realised he was wearing a ring that was almost identical to my own. It was a lot chunkier than mine, and it was made of a darker metal than the silver band that twisted around my own finger. But, they were unmistakably a matching pair.

I pressed my palm against his and examined both of our ringed fingers, in awe.

"You know, when I first saw that box, I panicked because I thought there was going to be an engagement ring in there," I confessed.

He laughed softly. "Not really my style, love."

I kept my palm pressed against his, and my lip twitched in a teasing smile. "You not the marrying kind, Mr Harris?"

His eyes darkened, and his hand curled down over mine, until our fingers were twined together.

"Your soul is bonded to mine by a link that has existed for thousands of years. I don't need a piece of paper to tell me that I am as bound to you as I could ever possibly be, love."

I shivered as cool, blue fire ran from his hand to mine. I looked down at our intertwined fingers and frowned.

"Lyall, are you sharing your energy with me by force?"

Stepping back from me and dropping my hand, he smiled grimly. "Just a little insurance policy, love. I didn't trust you to keep taking the help you needed when the time came."

My hand flew to the silver band on my hand, but he quickly laid his fingers over mine to stop me.

"It's not the ring that lets me do it, love. I've been practising ever since I knew you wouldn't be able to see it through."

"So, you're going to kill yourself?" I said coldly.

He smiled crookedly. "I told you before, I'm gonna save the girl and the world."

"And what happens then, Lyall? Did you forget that because we're bonded, I'm probably gonna either die of grief, or go completely mad if I lose you?" I snarled.

He reached forward and pressed the tip of his index finger gently against the centre of my chest.

"I know what's in here, love. I can feel it. You're stronger than you know and braver than you think. You'll survive it. I know you will."

"I think you're forgetting one important thing," I said.

He waited expectantly for me to continue.

"Right now, I want to survive because I have you. If you're

gone then I don't want to survive, Lyall. I'll let go. I won't fight it anymore." I folded my arms across my chest.

He shrugged. "I'll take that chance, love. It's still better than any of the alternatives."

We both stood and stared defiantly at each other.

Before either of us could say anything else, Bear's voice cut through the tension surrounding us.

"They're back. They're both back."

Once Artair and Freya were back in human form, they filled us in on everything they had seen from above the castle.

"He doesn't care." Artair shook his head in disbelief as he spoke. "Every gate and every door is open and unguarded. He's just waiting for us to walk right in."

"He's not afraid of us," I said softly.

"Which means he thinks he's got the upper hand," Bear mused.

"With two hundred Supers on his side, he *does* have the upper hand." Freya shrugged.

Lyall turned to Artair. "Call Enid and find out how long until she gets here." Looking back to all of us, he continued. "If he's expecting us, then we have no surprise element left. There's no point in waiting any longer, as soon as Enid and the animal souls arrive, we'll attack. We have nothing to lose."

I blinked slowly. *I have everything to lose.*

Bear nodded grimly. "About time, it's the waiting that puts me on edge."

Freya stood and looked up at the sun, which was peeking

through the treetops as midday quickly approached.

"Well, at least by the end of the day, we'll finally know who's gonna win this war."

CHAPTER
35

Enid arrived forty minutes after her final conversation with Artair. The animal souls poured through the woodland and surrounded us with myriad colours. They were beautiful to look at, glistening and sparkling, almost as though they were made of ice but ice that was every single colour of the rainbow.

Enid and Artair shared a quick hug before they joined our circle. This was our final war council before we attacked. I glanced around at the faces of each of my Dion.

This is probably the last time we will all stand together.

"There's no way of making this sound any better than it is," Lyall admitted. "Sluag knows we're coming, and he knows he's better prepared than we are. Our only hope is to fight him and the Supers off for long enough that Flora can get his soul out of his body and in the box."

I pursed my lips as Lyall spoke. He hadn't told the other Dion he was planning on feeding me every drop of his energy until he was dead.

Finlay stood next to Lyall. "Enid, do the animal souls know how they are to be split up?"

Enid nodded. "Yes, half will be fighting the Supers and half will protect Flora and Lyall, at all costs."

"The Draugur are all briefed to simply disarm as many Supers as possible. As soon as we win access to the cellars beneath the castle, we can start locking them away," Artair said confidently.

Satisfied, Lyall nodded. "Then I think we're ready to move."

"Not quite." I stepped into the centre of the circle, determined to voice what was on my mind.

"I still can't help but feel as though none of you would be in this situation if it wasn't for me."

Several of my Dion started to talk, but I held up a hand to silence them before continuing.

"I know that you all understand what your job as Dion means, and I know that each and every one of you will lay down your lives willingly today, if it means defeating Sluag and protecting the mortal world from ruin."

I looked around me and licked my lips. I felt parched all of a sudden.

"I want you to know that as your Soul Keeper, I am prepared to do exactly the same. I'm not afraid to die, as long as it means that this day finishes up with Sluag inside this box."

My hand automatically found the Síorraidh box at my hip and held on to it tightly. Lyall looked as though he was going to speak, so I rushed on.

"I don't want any of you to give your lives for me today, I've never wanted any of you to die for me. Including Mara." I gave Artair a sorrowful look, and he nodded back to me.

"I never wanted any of you to sacrifice yourselves for me." I looked at Finlay now, holding his gaze.

"All I ask from each of you is that you do everything in your power to help me get Sluag out of his body and locked away from this world, forever."

Finlay understood I was speaking directly to him. He knew what I was asking and he nodded once.

"Then let's do this." My voice came out as a whisper, but the Dion heard me, and we started the march on to Castle Dion.

Lyall caught up with me and matched his pace to mine. "Nice speech, love."

I shot him a sideways glance. "Thanks, I learned from the best."

As the castle walls came into view, I felt a shiver of fear. If anyone had told me a year ago that I would be marching to war at Castle Dion today, I would have laughed hard enough to rupture my spleen.

Soul Keeper or not, I was twenty years old, and I was completely terrified of what was going to happen next.

Suddenly, Finlay appeared at my right-hand side. Lyall was still walking next to me, on my left.

"Don't worry, Flor. Always and forever, remember?" Finlay's grin caused a smile to break out on my own face.

Lyall let his fingertips gently brush against my own as we

walked, pulling my attention back to him.

"I'm right by your side, love. I'm not going anywhere."

And just like that, my fear evaporated. My ragged breathing first slowed, before eventually quieting. I focussed my eyes forward and marched with certainty. With my best friend on one side and my soul mate on the other, I was indestructible. Sluag didn't stand a chance.

Understanding that we were never going to stage a surprise attack on Sluag, an unspoken agreement passed between us, and we headed straight for the main gate of Castle Dion.

We might as well do this with style.

As we passed beneath the cracked and crumbling archway that led into the gardens, I was devastated to see the destruction that Sluag and his Draugur had wreaked on the castle in such a short space of time.

As we had predicted, the fire hadn't damaged any of the stonework but the beautiful, old stones were covered in soot and smoke marks, giving the castle an air of darkness and despair.

The gardens were a scorched wasteland that wrapped around the hulking black towers of Castle Dion. The ornamental pond, which had been painstakingly maintained by Pen, was choked with weeds and muddied with soil that had been poured into the once crystal waters.

No trees remained. Every single one had been cut down and removed. Only a chessboard of stumps stretched out into the distance, the last proof that anything had ever lived here before.

Sluag stood in the centre of the ruined land—his Supers and mortal world Draugur alike flanked him. They were a terrifying and formidable army.

Sluag had paid particular attention to his clothing today, it seemed. As I walked forward, closing the gap between us, I noticed that he was bedecked in full grey armour, from head to toe.

His long, grey cloak blew about his imposing frame in the surprisingly cold wind. He no longer wore a short dress-sword at his hip; it had been replaced by a full-sized claymore that extended up in front of him, from the pointed tip which was buried in the soil at his feet. Sluag leaned on the hilt—which was level with his chest—with both arms as he watched me approaching him through hooded eyes.

My blood ran cold as I surveyed the scene, quickly realising that this was exactly how my dream had started out. Everything looked the same and sounded the same. I was standing in the same place, and eventually Sluag would raise his arm and slash it through the air to signal the start of the attack to his eagerly waiting Supers and Draugur.

I heard a snarl next to me and a shriek above my head. I snapped back to the present and suddenly realised all of my Dion had shifted ready for battle. All of them, except Lyall and Finlay, who remained stonily silently at my side.

Bear stood up on his hind legs and bellowed with all of his ten-foot-tall vocal power and Artair, Enid, and Freya circled above our heads, calling out their own primal challenge to Sluag.

Finlay shot me an apologetic glance. "I can't change, Flor."

"I know, your body is moments from failing right now," I murmured absently.

"How did you know that?" Finlay asked as he and Lyall both stared at me in surprise.

"Because I've been here before," I growled before taking a halting step forward to address the creature from my nightmare.

CHAPTER 36

"And so, we are finally come to this long-awaited moment in time, Little Dreamer."

Sluag handed the claymore to one of his minions and spread his arms wide, as though to encompass as much of the scene before him as possible. Taking a step forward, Sluag beckoned me to do the same.

I looked around me and considered it for a moment. We were still separated by around thirty metres. He couldn't touch me in the time it would take for me to be surrounded by my protectors. I lifted my foot and took two steps forward.

"And that's far enough," Lyall growled as he walked forward next to me. Finlay remained firmly at my other side.

Sluag's eyes sparkled as they looked from Finlay to Lyall. I could see him trying to decide which of my Dion he would target first.

"That's a nice ring you're wearing, Flora."

Ahh, so we're going after Lyall first.

"I didn't think jewellery was really your thing, Sluag." I was sure sass wasn't called for on the battlefield, but without my smart mouth, my arsenal was pretty empty.

He shook his head and grinned, exposing his rows of yellowing teeth. "It isn't, especially when it is given as a promise that will ultimately be broken."

I rolled my eyes, not about to give Sluag the satisfaction of a reply.

"There'll be no promises broken here today, Sluag. Flora will walk away from this, and I will have kept the only promise that matters." Lyall's voice lashed out across the field.

"A noble fool until the bitter end, Lyall. Honestly, I will feel remorse when your broken body lies at my feet." Sluag shrugged his shoulders at Lyall before shifting his gaze back to mine.

I felt an uncomfortable prodding inside my head and realised Sluag was trying to steal our battle plan from inside my head. I quickly concentrated on slamming the shutters of my mind closed, and I felt him recoil quickly.

"Your little mind thefts don't work in the mortal world, Sluag," I spat.

Finlay suddenly groaned next to me, and I shot him a concerned glance. He lifted his hand to his head and pressed the temple as though he had a migraine.

"I think it might be time to jump ship, Flor," he murmured.

Not wanting to give Sluag any idea of what we had planned, I whispered back to him frantically. "Not just yet, Finlay. Five minutes and it'll be time."

Sluag raised his sparse, grey eyebrows and smirked.

"Looks to me like your Dion is about to find himself without a body again, Flora."

I shrugged. "It's only what you told me would happen, Sluag. Anyway, if we're all going to be dead in a few minutes, it doesn't really matter, right?"

Sluag narrowed his eyes as he studied my face. He knew that he was close to uncovering some sort of information, but he couldn't quite put his finger on exactly what.

I shrouded my mind, fearful he would try his smash and grab tactics to get hold of the longed-for intelligence that could help him avoid the Síorraidh box. As I thought of the box, my hand automatically went to my hip and came to rest against the coolness of the carved wood.

"Time's almost up, Finlay," Sluag grinned.

Finlay lifted his head and glared at the scaly monster.

"That body is going to fall apart at any moment, and once it does there is nowhere left for you to go. You have exhausted all possible options available to you." Sluag took another step toward us.

"I'd rather die and be reincarnated than spend an eternity trapped inside a tiny box," Finlay gloated. "The future isn't exactly looking rosy for you either, Sluag."

"Let's be honest, we all know I'm not going inside that box. Our little Soul Keeper doesn't have the power to put me there." Sluag laid his bony hand over the place in his chest where his heart would be, if he had one.

"And, yes, I know she can draw on loyal Lyall's energy too. However, I'm quietly confident that Flora doesn't have the guts to kill her soul mate. Do you, Little Dreamer?"

I hesitated for the briefest instant, and in that moment, Sluag looked through my face and into the very core of my soul. I felt the burn of his eyes as he invaded the sanctuary of my whole inner-being and saw through my charade as though it were made of glass, to recognise the absolute truth of my very existence.

I felt the blackness of his own soul twist its threads in glee as it realised I could never sacrifice Lyall, not even to save the world.

Suddenly, Sluag bombarded me with images of hospitals burning, dead-eyed zombie people wandering aimlessly through streets that were crumbling and broken. Children that were orphaned and dying, and not one single person cared.

It was heartbreaking.

I choked and staggered back from the weight of the visions he threw at me. But, my greatest sorrow was fed by the abject shame of knowing that, even now, I still couldn't sacrifice Lyall.

Sluag's eyes widened in surprise and delight as he stole my truth.

"Flora Bast, you are going to be the greatest disappointment this world has ever known."

I couldn't speak; there was nothing to say. My own stupid weakness was going to kill everyone here. My mind ran frantic with questions and regrets.

Why did I bring them here to die?

Lyall touched his hand to mine, and I flinched back from him. "What's wrong, love? What's he doing to you?"

I shook my head frantically, certain the shame that burned on my face would give me away as a coward to Lyall and to everyone watching.

Sluag clapped his hands together, and his army of Supers and Draugur stamped their feet and straightened their backs. They were spoiling for this fight.

"I must confess myself disappointed, Little Dreamer. I was rooting for you, I really was. I still think you will always be my favourite Soul Keeper. Almost like the daughter I never really got the chance to know."

Lyall tried again. "Flora, are you okay?"

Bracing myself for what was to come, I nodded to him once. "I will be. We have to put him in that box, Lyall." I shuddered. "The alternative just isn't an option."

"Flora?" Finlay's voice was shaky. I turned around in just enough time to see the Super Draugur body split entirely in half, as though it had been hit by a bolt of lightning.

The bright white Finlay soul was ejected from the body of the Super, before spiralling up into the air in front of me, and just like that, my best friend was out of options.

"Finlay?" I called out, terrified that he would be lost in limbo in the mortal world.

I'm okay, Flor. I just hope your plan's gonna work.

"So, do I," I muttered.

"Well, Little Dreamer." Sluag's voice pulled my attention back toward the Host of the Unforgiven Dead and the nightmarish army that stood at his back.

Sluag had returned to the place he first stood when we started talking. He held out his hand and retrieved his sword from the Super that had been holding it steady while its master engaged in his theatrics.

I felt a tremor of déjà vu as I faced Sluag. My mind flashing back to the horror of my dream, once again.

Sluag continued to stare at me with his fire-pit eyes as he spoke.

"Time is up. The final battle is here, and I will watch each and every one of you fall down in flames. I tried to reason with you, Flora. What happens next is all on you. Every last drop of blood is your responsibility."

I held his gaze defiantly as I drew my own short sword and pointed it in his direction. There was nowhere left to hide.

"Then let's do it," I said softly.

Sluag nodded once, never taking his eyes from mine.

"Attack," he howled.

And they did.

CHAPTER 37

I'm pretty sure that when they show you the great and final battle scenes on TV shows, they always slow down that first, initial clash of the warring sides. The two opponents rush toward each other at a digitally reduced speed that allows the viewer to comprehend everything that unfolds—step by violent step.

What I hadn't realised was that the first thirty-seconds of a real battle feels exactly the same way. As Sluag's arm slashed down through the air in perfect synchronisation with his call to arms, I inhaled a deep and cleansing breath.

Sluag's entire army began to surge forward as though they were the waves of an ocean, desperate to crash and break apart against the shore. I could see the steely determination on each face as they started to build up speed in their approach. They had one goal and one goal only—to tear me and my army apart.

I turned slowly, as though I were inside my nightmare all over again, and looked to the faces of those who were on my side of the fight.

The two eagles and the raven above our heads each called out one final shriek of defiance before they pitched into a long, slow dive toward the upturned faces of their enemies waiting below.

The Draugur that had sworn their loyalty to me because of my blood, marched forward unblinkingly. Their faces gave no emotions away because beneath the false, human husks, they didn't have any. These were the same monsters that were coming to kill us. The only difference was, they had been forced to change their allegiance to me.

Although the quiet and determined march of the loyal Draugur unnerved me, I was grateful for them. Without my own army of monsters, I would never have been able to buy enough time to do what was needed to end this fight.

An earth-shattering roar brought my attention to Bear. He had pulled himself up to his maximum height before releasing the animalistic battle-cry. As I stared, the massive brown bear let itself drop onto all four paws, and the ground shook. Bear didn't hesitate, and for such a big animal, he had surprising grace as he sprang forward and galloped toward the nearest Super.

The bright white Finlay light hovered above my head; without a body he was unable to engage in any fighting. I permitted myself a brief moment of relief that he was out of the body of the Super. Communicating with Finlay alone would be a lot easier now he was back in soul form, and I had things I needed to say to him that I didn't want other ears to hear.

I looked toward the colourful army of animal souls as they leaped into action and started to split into two separate groups. They moved with absolute certainty in each other, and their grace and synchronicity was beautiful to watch.

The first group peeled off from the main body of animal souls and began to create a spearhead formation that approached Sluag's horde on the right-hand side, pushing them closer together and driving them into my marching Draugur.

The second group of animal souls wheeled around and fanned out into a protective semi-circle that created the perfect barrier between myself and the rest of Sluag's army. The shining animals then walked themselves slowly backward, until they were as tightly knit in front of Lyall and I as they could get.

Lastly, my eyes landed on the dark-haired Dion who stood next to me. He watched the animal souls form around us, and I could sense the shame that burned inside him. He hated being kept from the battle while the other Dion risked their lives. He wanted to do his job. He wanted to fight. But, that wasn't why he was here. I needed his help to put an end to this, but only for as long as it wouldn't kill him.

A loud sound drew my attention back to the main battlefield just in time to see Bear collide with the first Super Draugur. He was quickly followed by the other warriors at the front-line of my army, and just like that, the slow-motion build up ended.

The first thing that changed was the volume of the fight. Everything became loud, almost unbearably so. The speed with which everything happened accelerated rapidly to a point that meant I couldn't even follow half of the action with my eyes as it unfolded.

The breathtaking beauty of Enid's animal souls belied how vicious they could be when needed. The animals attacked the Supers and mortal world Draugur with absolute ferocity, and it quickly became apparent they were impossible to predict because each different animal made the most of its own skills when it attacked.

One minute a Super could be fighting a shining, green cobra that would strike at its face with unnatural speed. In the next moment, it would be defending itself against the teeth and claws of a bright orange jaguar that was intent on removing the Supers throat.

Even though I was struggling to follow the fight now that everything had sped up so much, I knew one thing for certain; we were holding our own. Quick surveillance of the battlefield told me this was no longer going to be the whitewash I had despaired over time and time again.

As my eyes moved over the fighting, they were suddenly captured by the burning oil-slicks set within Sluag's grey, scaled face. He stared at me, and I stared back defiantly. I could sense his fury over how the fight had begun; this was not what he had expected.

It was now impossible to speak, or to hear someone speak, over the deafening roar of battle, so I didn't waste my breath. I simply gave Sluag a cold, hard smile of triumph. I knew the battle was far from won, but it hadn't been a bad start and for now, that was enough.

I felt Lyall touch his fingers against mine, and a jolt of fire teased around my hand and wrist.

"It's time to keep up our end of the deal, love," he said loud enough that I could just hear him over the din.

I couldn't resist one last glance back to where Sluag stood. He was as far back from the front-line as he could be. None of my army had a chance of laying a single finger on him. His Supers and mortal world Draugur were starting to fall all around him, but he didn't blink. He had the air of a commander who would sacrifice each and every soul who fought for him without hesitation or regret.

I shook my head in disgust, knowing he would understand the thought that was running through my mind.

Coward.

Sluag didn't respond to my insult in the way I had expected. He slowly shook his head from side to side. A wide grin split his face, revealing the rows of his yellow tombstone teeth. Leaving one hand to rest on the hilt of his sword, Sluag haltingly lifted his other hand up until it was extended before him.

He tucked each of the bony fingers of his hand into his palm until just his index finger remained, pointing in a fixed direction. My gaze travelled the invisible line that extended from his finger until my eyes landed on Lyall's face.

"Flora, we need to crack on." Lyall spoke with urgency.

I nodded and reached out to take Lyall's hand in my own.

Shifting my gaze back to Sluag, I shuddered as he stopped pointing at Lyall. Lifting his arm even higher, until it was level with his shoulder, he slowly and deliberately drew his hand across the air in front of his throat. The grin never leaving his rotten face.

His intent was clear.

Lyall will die.

CHAPTER 38

Giving my hand a gentle tug, Lyall brought my attention fully back to him.

"Okay, I'm ready." I spoke with a confidence I didn't feel.

I kept my fingers firmly entwined with Lyall's. No matter what else happened, we had to keep touching for as long as I needed to draw on his energy.

Turning back to face Sluag, I focussed all of my concentration on him as I pushed past the boundaries of the physical, allowing my soul to burrow its way past his body and into the cavity inside him that housed his black and rotting soul.

Sluag's eyes widened imperceptibly as he felt the push of my own soul against his. *He hadn't realised how powerful I had become.*

Smiling grimly at my small success, I concentrated on allowing the strands of my own soul to wrap around his. I needed to anchor myself against him so that when I called his soul forward, I had the ability to reel his out like a fish.

I felt a vague sense of surprise and delight as I realised for the first time that my own soul was a vivid purple colour.

Allowing my concentration to drop—even momentarily—was a mistake. A single hard push ejected my soul from Sluag's body in an instant and sent my mortal body reeling backward with the force. Only Lyall's unending grip prevented me from losing my footing and landing on my ass.

Raising a brow, Lyall smiled. "Time to call in the reinforcements, Soul Keeper."

I nodded breathlessly as I rounded on Sluag and prepared for my second attempt. Inside my head, I called out to my best friend.

Finlay, it's time.

The little white orb had been bobbing patiently at a safe distance, but it didn't hesitate when I called.

What do you want me to do, Flor?

I looked to Sluag and was surprised to see he looked more than a little worried.

I was going to try to do this in stages, Finlay, but he's too strong, too ancient. Let's just go for it.

The white light fired across the battleground so quickly he left a trail of magnesium-bright light behind him.

All the way? Finlay checked with me in the instant before he collided with Sluag's broad chest.

I swallowed back my fear. *All the way.*

As Finlay crashed into Sluag he started to melt, first through the armour and then through the monster's grey scaled skin. Sluag howled in anger and fear.

Gripping Lyall's hand tightly in my own, I shouted so he could hear me over the noises that surrounded us.

"It's going to be just like we did with the Super, Lyall. Finlay will get inside and push, we need to pull as though our lives depend on it."

Lyall frowned for a moment. "What happens to Finlay once Sluag's soul is out, love?"

I had a pretty good idea—at least I hoped I did. But that could wait until after we'd won.

"Not important, Lyall. If you really want to do this, then let's do it," I shouted.

He only hesitated for a moment, and then I felt the warm flow of his energy passing through his own hand and into mine. The fire flicked and curled up my wrist and then climbed up my arm. It felt as though I were being supercharged.

I smiled gratefully at him before turning swiftly back to focus all of my attention on Sluag's writhing form.

I felt myself become overrun with energy from Lyall, to the point that it was almost painful. I concentrated on twining Lyall's energy with my own. The end result, a kaleidoscope of colours containing a bolt of power that would have been strong enough to take down a whole herd of elephants.

As I raised my hand with the palm facing Sluag, I didn't even have to encourage the energy bolt. Without hesitation, it leapt from my hand in an arc of blue fire and punched its way through Sluag's chest.

He roared in fury, as for the first time ever, he truly understood exactly how much power I had when my soul mate and my best friend stood beside me.

As the blue fire found its way into the pit that surrounded Sluag's soul, I felt Finlay pressing against the black mass. I could almost see my best friend with his shoulder braced against Sluag, his head down, and his face red with the exertion of trying to eject the immortal soul from its millennia-aged body.

My initial elation was short-lived. I felt Finlay tremble as Sluag pushed back against him. Finlay's soul snapped back like an elastic band, and for a terrifying moment, I was sure he had been obliterated somehow.

Finlay? I called out desperately, inside my mind.

I'm okay, Flor. He didn't get me out, just gave me a slap is all.

I sighed in relief at the sound of my best friend's voice inside my head.

"Again," I snarled aloud, as I threw my energy against Sluag for a second time.

Finlay started to push once more, and I closed my eyes as I concentrated on firing every drop of power inside me across the battlefield and into the body of the creature I had to stop at all costs.

Sluag roared in fear, and I pushed and pushed. Even when I could hear Finlay inside my head, screaming at me to stop, I carried on.

Only when a firm hand gripped my chin, and I heard Lyall's

voice shouting at me, did I snap back to the present.

"Flora, enough. You're going to kill yourself."

I blinked slowly as I stared into Lyall's amber eyes. I lifted the back of my hand to my nose. When I pulled my hand away, I was horrified to see, not the usual trickle of blood but a river of it, running across the back of my hand.

Lyall touched the back of his hand gently to my cheek.

"You have to take more from me, love. I have plenty left to give, yet."

"No. You'll die," I growled.

"Flora, you don't have the power to do it alone, and right now Finlay is trapped inside that thing, along with the darkest soul in the history of humanity. You can't do it without me, love."

He was right. *Dammit, I didn't want him to be right.*

"Okay." I wiped the blood from my face and ignored the stabbing pain inside my head.

Lyall wrapped his hand around mine and smiled down at me. I looked back at him and felt as though I were being torn in two. Indecision raged through me.

Finlay, we're going to go again. I called out to my best friend.

I'm ready when you are, Flor. Even though his voice was inside my head, I knew he was grinding the words out around clenched teeth.

I fixed my attention on the warm tingles of energy that kissed my fingers as they leapt from Lyall's skin. I concentrated on soaking up all of the energy that Lyall was offering, absorbing it into myself. My own body becoming a conduit that would collect his energy and merge it with my own, before sending the blue fire back after Sluag's soul again.

My eyes met Sluag's once more, and this time he had the confidence to smile and shake his head slowly at me.

You can't do this, Little Dreamer.

I dropped my gaze and focused on the blue fire that crackled and burned across my open palm.

Finlay, now, I yelled inside my head.

As the blue fire bled from my hand and ate its way through Sluag's chest for the second time, I felt Finlay respond to my call. He pushed against the dark orb inside Sluag. I felt my flame of energy retreat a minute amount, as Sluag's soul began to shift toward the entry point of my power.

"It's working," I shouted in relief and delight.

Suddenly, Lyall grunted and fell to his knees beside me.

The terror of losing my soul mate was enough to make me drop my concentration and once again, my energy snapped back out of Sluag, leaving his soul unmoved.

Finlay cursed in frustration, but I ignored him, instead dropping to my knees beside Lyall. He looked up at me and frowned.

"No, Flora. We have to keep going. You know the deal."

I shook my head furiously. "I didn't make any deal."

He laughed weakly. "You're the Soul Keeper, love. The deal was made on your behalf, and you have to honour it."

I looked out across the raging battle, once again torn by

indecision.

Finally deciding, I stood up. "No, I don't."

Lyall started to speak, but he was quickly silenced as I brought the hilt of my sword down against the back of his skull.

There was no time to wonder if it would render him perfectly unconscious, like it did in the movies. I stood up quickly. I had to try to finish this.

I could feel Finlay's disbelief as I spoke to him inside my mind.

Finlay, again.

Suddenly, a voice raised in a sound of high-pitched elation above the noise of the battle. Sluag's laughter was so loud and gleeful that those closest to him stopped fighting and turned to look at him

"Oh, Flora," he shouted in delight. "What have you done?"

CHAPTER 39

Biting my lip, I stared around at the raging battle and tried to quash the bubbling self-hatred that threatened to overwhelm me. I saw each of my Dion surrounded by monstrosities that could not die. Bear was lashing out with his massive paws at the Supers who kept on coming at him in continuous waves of evil.

Freya was doing her best to help him by diving at the Supers and other Draugur, clawing at eyes with her talons. She had clearly been in a few close scrapes because her feathers were looking a little ragged around the edges.

Artair and Enid never left each other alone for a minute; the two eagles attacked in tandem. Their perfectly aligned aerial displays made them seem formidable and untouchable. But, I knew the truth. I'd learned it the hard way and so had Artair. They could easily die, and I had just made a decision that meant they probably would.

Flora? Finlay's voice sounded desperate inside my head.

Okay. Again, Finlay. I faced Sluag and prepared myself to

attack.

His voice was sceptical. *Flor, we can't do this without Lyall.*

Glancing down at Lyall's unconscious form, I stood firm and prepared to send my own energy across the battlefield toward Sluag again.

We don't have a choice, Finlay.

Not anymore, we don't, Flora.

I heard the disappointment in his voice, and it hurt like hell, but there was no time to dwell on it now.

My energy leapt back into Sluag once more, and my soul gripped on to Sluag's. Finlay steeled himself before starting to push against the corrupt, black orb in another attempt to dislodge it from the void inside the Host of the Unforgiven Dead.

After only seconds had passed, my whole body burned with a need to pull my soul back and stop haemorrhaging any more energy. I ignored the burn and kept on pushing, even as my vision started to dull and a splitting white-hot headache pierced my brain.

Finlay howled with the sheer exertion of pushing against a soul that was thousands of years more ancient than him.

I reached out for Finlay's soul with my own, terrified that Sluag would destroy him, but the tiny white light was holding its own impressively.

I could feel Sluag's soul starting to vacate the cavity inside him. He was struggling to hold fast against our power. With hope renewed, I threw everything I had at him, and his armoured body thrashed and kicked in anger as he realised he was losing his grip.

I could suddenly taste the river of blood which had begun to cascade down over my lips, and the battle started to sound farther and farther away as my senses began to shut down. I was dying and I knew it. But that was okay because Lyall would wake up, and he would live, and I would have fulfilled my duty as Soul Keeper.

I couldn't stop myself from dropping to my knees once more as my legs gave way beneath me. I could hear my heartbeat inside my own ears now, and it was slow, so very slow.

Flora? Finlay howled.

I'm okay, keep going, I replied groggily. I pushed my energy against Sluag's soul once again.

That was when something truly miraculous happened.

As I sent what I suspected was the final burst of energy I had left in me toward Sluag, I felt a huge surge of flame that engulfed my own power and carried it across the battlefield. The blue fire ripped through Sluag's chest with such force it punched his black and rotten soul straight through his back and out into the open air.

Freya? I spoke weakly inside my head.

The raven didn't hesitate; she dived toward me and hooked her beak through the loop that held the Síorraidh box on my belt, tearing it away from me.

Freya shot back up into the sky until she became a tiny speck against the blue expanse. Then she opened her beak and let the box fall toward the earth.

As the box tumbled and spun, I felt the roar of anger and fear that emanated from the inky, black Sluag soul.

This is not the end for me, Flora. I won't go in that box. His voice was malevolent and threatening.

As the box completed its final revolution in the air, it landed with a cracking sound against a rock that protruded from the ground. As the box hit the rock, the lid sprang open, and a tortured scream ripped through my mind as Sluag's soul was pulled into the blue, wooden box before the lid clicked quickly closed again.

I had somehow ended up lying down on the floor with my face pressed against the damp straw-coloured grass. My vision was fading in and out, but I saw enough to know that Sluag was done.

"Yes, you will go in that box," I murmured around the blood that tainted my mouth with copper as I let my eyes drift closed.

A sudden thought jolted me back from the brink of unconsciousness, and my eyes opened in just enough time to see Sluag's body sitting up from the prone position it had adopted when the tainted, black soul had been ejected from it.

Sluag stood up and started to walk shakily across the battlefield, toward where I lay. The fighting still raged around him. The Supers weren't quite ready to back down yet, it seemed.

I managed to lift my head up from the grass a fraction as Sluag approached me. Once he was standing with his grey boots only inches from my face, he dropped into a crouch and peered down until his fire-pit eyes met my green ones.

I grinned, despite the pain inside my head.

"You do know you can choose any shape, now. I hope you're not planning on sticking with that one," I croaked.

A slow smile spread across his grey scaly face, only all of a sudden, it wasn't quite so scaly any more. The features began to swim and change, in much the same way the face of the first Draugur I ever met had done, all those months ago.

The sparse, grey hair became lighter and thicker, and the fire within his eyes died back until they ended up a sparkling blue colour. His skin paled and the scales disappeared, until I was finally looking at the face of my best friend.

He spoke slowly, as though hearing his voice for the very first time. "It's good to be back, Flor."

"It's really good to have you back, Finlay Michaelson." I smiled through my tears.

The sounds of fighting returned to my ears, and I gave Finlay a weak but urgent push.

"A blood inheritance secures allegiance. Go on, those Supers belong to you now. Stop them?"

He stood up and looked hesitantly at me.

"Go on, end this," I urged as I started to pull myself up.

"The ones that were made with my blood will listen, but not the ones made with Pen's blood, Flor," he insisted.

"Do it," I growled as I fought to sit up.

Finlay coughed to clear his throat before calling out, "Super Draugur, kneel."

It was as though a magic spell had been cast over them, and perhaps in a way, it had. Each and every Super turned toward the sound of Finlay's voice and without hesitation, they dropped to one knee and bowed their heads in deference.

"My Lord," they murmured in unison.

Finlay turned astonished eyes on me. "They all knelt, even Pen's Supers. Why?"

I fought back tears as I finally admitted the truth to my best friend.

"I didn't want to tell you before in case the soul in the Everwood was wrong. But it wasn't. Pen was your mother, Finlay. She never once pretended to be your mother in all those years, because you really are her son."

He blinked in shock. "A blood inheritance secures allegiance," he murmured.

I nodded. "Yep, Pen's Draugur inherited the exact same blood as you did."

CHAPTER
40

The battle was won. The mortal world Draugur threw down their weapons and surrendered as soon as they saw their stronger cousins kneeling before Finlay.

My Dion quickly shifted back into human shape and began embracing each other in celebration and delight. Sluag was in the Síorraidh box, and we were all still alive.

Finlay had begun leading the Supers to the cellars of Castle Dion—better safe than sorry. We had no idea if they might decide to go rogue again, and the cellars were a good place to keep them under control until they could be returned to the Endwood.

I had begun to feel a little better, and I knew I needed to apologise to Lyall for what I had done. I knelt beside him and gently touched my hand to his cheek. It was ice cold and I had to stop myself from recoiling in shock.

"Lyall," I whispered, suddenly afraid.

He didn't reply, and my hands frantically sought the pulse-point in his neck. There wasn't even a weak pulse, and he wasn't breathing.

"Lyall," I cried.

This time the other Dion heard me and ran to my side.

"Flora, what is it?" Freya dropped to her knees next to me and held the back of her hand over Lyall's blue lips. She was trying to feel for breath.

I struggled to find enough of my own breath to speak. "He's not breathing, Freya. He's dead. How is he dead?"

Artair was kneeling at Lyall's head now. He studied my dark-haired Dion's face before gently hooking his fingers under Lyall's right hand, which was extended out from his body as though he had been reaching for something when he died.

"Flora, lift up the bottom of your jeans," Artair instructed me.

Choking back tears, I did as he asked and gasped when I saw a pale blue handprint against my ankle.

"I don't understand," I sobbed.

"I do," Freya said softly.

I turned toward her. My heart hurt so much I could barely breathe.

Freya frowned sadly. "He woke up and knew you wouldn't accept his help. So, he did it without you knowing, Flora. I don't know how he managed to force you to take his energy, but I think that's what he did."

I thought back to the way my palm had pressed against his, just before we marched on Castle Dion. His energy had flickered around my fingertips even though I had tried to stop him from sharing it with me.

Just a little insurance policy, love.

I bowed my head over his chest, and the tears escaped me. He'd known I wouldn't be able to do it, and he'd made sure that when the time came, I wouldn't have a choice.

I thought back to when the bolt of extra energy had surged through me. I should have realised it wasn't a miracle—miracles don't happen. Lyall had given every single piece of himself. He had sacrificed himself, to make sure he stopped Sluag and saved my life. My mind was suddenly filled with the image of his crooked smile.

I'm gonna save the girl and the world.

Finding his cold hand and wrapping it in my own, I shook my head over and over again, denying that my soul mate was truly dead.

"What have you done?" I whispered. "What have you done?"

Grief completely overwhelmed me. I bent my head until my forehead came to rest on the familiar black T-shirt that covered his chest. I kept trying to form words to tell him how angry I was with him, but all I could do was let the tears fall with such ferocity I didn't think they would ever stop.

The other Dion stood up and took a few steps back as though to give me some privacy. Each of them had bowed heads and tears staining their cheeks.

I finally managed to speak.

"I told you not to leave me, Lyall Harris. You promised me what we have is eternal. It goes beyond even this. I can't live unless you're there with me," I whispered brokenly.

As I spoke, I could feel the truth of my words, and I began to really understand what it was for a Soul Keeper to lose a bonded Dion. My body might have started to shut down when I used too much energy in the fight against Sluag, but this was something completely different.

I had never even felt the stirrings of my soul trying to shut down before. I hadn't truly known it was possible.

Now I did. It was as though my soul was a caged bird that had been deliriously happy inside its gilt prison until it realised there was a whole other world out there, that it had never even known existed.

Once the bird had a taste of how exquisite that big wide world was, it wanted out, and it was content to die trying. The bird would keep on flying into the bars of its cage, until its body was a battered and broken mess—because in truth, even that was better than the alternative.

My soul was the bird, and it flew against the cage of my chest over and over again, breaking apart a little more with each desperate collision. It was determined that it would continue doing so until I died, because a life without Lyall, was no life at all.

I vaguely registered the sound of Finlay's voice, and even that brought me no solace. Even though for months now, I had been desperate to hear Finlay's real voice again, instead of the strange tone his Super body had used. I heard him from a thousand miles away. I was just a temporary spectator here, waiting to die.

"What happened?" Finlay.

"It's Lyall, he's gone." Artair.

"No, he can't be." Finlay.

I felt Finlay kneel next to me and his arm wrapped around my trembling shoulders. "Flora, it's going to be okay. I promise you it's going to be okay."

It didn't matter. My soul was almost done. It only needed to crash into those bars just a couple more times, and I would be free—my soul would be free.

I tried to tell Finlay that it was okay, that I was dead now. But he wasn't talking to me any longer.

He had pulled a short blade from his hip, and I watched in horror as he drew it across his wrist. As the blood welled up in the channel of the wound I tried to cry out to him.

You're not supposed to die. It's me, I'm doing the dying, Finlay.

But he couldn't hear me, probably because I was nearly dead now, I thought.

He leaned over Lyall and started to let the crimson fluid drip into Lyall's slightly open mouth.

What are you doing? He's dead. Let him be, I screamed from inside my cage.

Finlay couldn't hear me, and he carried on letting the warm blood drip from his wrist into Lyall's mouth as I stared in horrified fascination.

"I don't know if this will work," he said to the other Dion. "I don't know how long he was gone."

My little bird was frantic now. No sooner did it pick itself up from the floor after its last failed attempt at freedom, than it would launch itself at the bars again, earning yet another broken bone. The bird wanted to protect Lyall. It had to protect him at all costs. All I could hear inside my mind was my own voice screaming and screaming for Finlay to stop.

And then there was silence.

The tears cleared from my eyes, and I was able to focus on the amber wolf-eyes that stared back at me.

My bird hesitated mid-flight, unsure if it was supposed to carry on trying to die.

"Lyall," I whispered.

"Hello, love." He blinked.

EPILOGUE

"Are you seriously bringing jelly?" I laughed.

"Damn straight, I'm bringing jelly. What sort of party doesn't have jelly?" Lyall's eyes grew more wolfish as he leaned forward and snaffled a miniature quiche from the cooling tray I had just placed on the kitchen counter.

I reached out, lightning quick and slapped the back of his hand.

"Ouch." He laughed as he collected the tray and headed for the cottage door.

Looking at the clock that my parents had fixed on to the kitchen wall when they very first moved in to this house—all those years ago—I swore under my breath.

"We're going to be late," I yelled.

"Why do you think I'm leaving, love." Lyall's voice trailed back through the open front door.

A yowl near my ankles caught my attention, and I looked down to see three hungry faces staring up at me.

"Okay, okay. I'll feed you before I go."

Achilles, Phobos, and Deimos purred appreciatively as I filled their bowls with food and quickly dropped them onto the floor.

"Now be good. I have somewhere I need to be."

When I reached the garden, I sighed in frustration. I couldn't believe Lyall had already gone. I gave one last glance around at the overgrown weeds and trees that still surrounded my parents' cottage—my cottage.

"I'll deal with it next week." I shrugged before imagining myself inside the Everwood.

As I materialised beneath the Síorraidh trees, I marvelled again at their new purple colour before setting off to catch up with Lyall.

My Everwood had been restored to its former glory since Sluag had been boxed for eternity, but it did have a few small differences. The colour of the flowers was one of them.

A few days after we had taken back Castle Dion, I had gone for a walk down to the shore of Loch Ness in the dead of night and taken the blue box with me.

Just before I hurled the Síorraidh box into the centre of the deep, green water, I had pressed my mouth against the crack of the lid.

"Your days of hurting people are over, monster. Sleep well."

I could have sworn that Sluag was screaming as the box arced through the air and splashed into the water to settle for an eternity within the depths of the loch.

I hurried through the trees, excited to see Finlay. I hadn't seen him for a while. My best friend was now technically Sluag's replacement. He was immortal—which took some getting used to. Although, if he hadn't inherited Sluag's immortal blood, then he would never have been able to bring Lyall back to me on the day of the battle.

So, I was more than grateful for Finlay's new status, but I was aware that it was taking him a little time to get used to his new role.

Finlay had free reign to come and go through both the Endwood and the Everwood it seemed.

According to Eric, it would stay that way unless I revoked his permission—which was never going to happen. Finlay was one of us, one of the good guys.

The Endwood looked completely different these days too. The trees were starting to grow back and they had recently begun to bloom with purple flowers, just like the ones in the Everwood. The dawn had remained to permanently replace the cold night sky that had roofed the Endwood for so many thousand years.

I stepped into a large clearing and found that my Dion had set up the mother of all parties. There were trestle tables laden with food and banners and bunting strung from every tree.

The animal souls were here in droves, and thousands of pure souls ducked and bobbed around me in delight as I walked across the clearing to greet my friends.

The rogue souls had all disappeared when Sluag was boxed, and we had no idea where they had gone. I was sure we hadn't seen the last of them, but it was nice to enjoy the respite for now.

Enid stood in the centre of the group, and she held a huge birthday cake that was alight with candles.

"Happy twenty-first birthday, Flora," she shouted happily.

I shook my head at Lyall, who stood next to Enid.

"Surprise." He smirked.

I blew out my candles and scowled at each of my friends, half-jokingly.

"I thought we said no birthday celebrations?"

Finlay stepped forward and wrapped me in a bear hug. "It's not a birthday celebration, Flor. It's a 'yay, you didn't get killed by a prophecy before your twenty-first birthday, celebration.' So that's okay."

"Smart ass." I laughed.

The party was surprisingly relaxed and exactly what I needed. It was amazing to spend time with each of my friends and not have to look over our shoulders every couple of minutes. I sat on a tree stump, alone for a moment while I studied the group.

It was going to take me a while before I stopped worrying about Finlay, but he seemed to be happy right now, and that was good enough, after everything we had been through.

I smiled at Artair and Enid as they sat, huddled together, deep in conversation. They were the perfect couple. Not like Bear and Freya, who fought like a cat and dog but always made up afterward.

"What you thinking about?" Finlay's voice made me jump

a fraction before I calmed down enough to gesture that he sit with me.

"If I said I was thinking about everything, you'd know what I mean, right?"

He nodded. "Yeah, I get that. You're doing okay, though, Flor?"

I smiled at him. "I'm doing fine. It's you I worry about."

"What, about me being the new Host of the Unforgiven Dead?" He laughed.

I shuddered. "We really need to give you a new title."

"How about just Finlay?"

"That'll do for now," I agreed.

Finlay stood up and headed toward the others. "I didn't get jelly. I'm so in need of jelly. Want some, Flor?"

I shook my head in frustration as Finlay headed back to the party. "We're adults. What is it with bloody jelly?" I growled.

"It's sweet," a voice whispered in my ear as strong arms wrapped around my waist from behind me.

I leaned back against Lyall and laughed. "Just like me, huh?"

"Well…" He shrugged and I punched his arm playfully.

"Have you had a nice time?" he murmured.

I thought about it before I answered. "Actually, I have."

"See, I told you birthday parties aren't that terrible." He stood up and pulled me against his chest.

He looked down into my eyes, before placing a gentle kiss against my lips. I pushed on to my toes and leaned into him before closing my eyes as I allowed myself to bask in the warmth of him. I felt a flicker of elation as my soul responded to his, and I felt thoroughly and wholly complete.

"I don't want any more, though," I grumbled, pulling back from him ever so slightly.

Leaning back in to kiss me again, he laughed softly. "I'm afraid that's non-negotiable, love"

THE END

THANK YOU

A thousand thank yous' to anybody who chose to pick up Soul Eternal, and read it. I am honoured that you gave me the opportunity to bring you along for the final part of Flora's journey. I really hope you enjoyed reading this trilogy as much as I enjoyed creating it.

Reviews are the life-blood of any Indie author, and I remain eternally grateful to those who leave a review for Soul Eternal after reading it. If you enjoyed the book, I'd be thrilled to know, and if not then please tell me what I could have done better. Feedback from readers is the best way for me to improve and grow as a writer.

Much love to you all. See you for the next series xxx

Please reach out to me. I love to hear from readers, and will always reply.

Facebook & Twitter: @AuthorKateKeir

Website: www.katekeir.com

ACKNOWLEDGEMENTS

A huge thanks to Katrina at Crimson Phoenix Creations for designing my beautiful book covers for all three books in the trilogy. You are so talented lady!

Thank you to my favourite ladies for reading the first draft of babble that I created, and telling me when I had got it right or wrong.

Thank you to my wonderful editor Lia. I can't believe you came back to edit three more of my books after the lengthy job you had with my debut. I would like to think I've improved a little since then, but thank you for polishing my manuscript up to publication standard.

Leigh, I am a nightmare. Thank you for your beautiful formatting skills, and your extreme patience.

To my long-suffering hubby, who had to endure writer's widowhood for six months while I wrote all three books, thank you for your unwavering support. I love you xxx